CW01214052

PAPER CHASE

Hugh Alexander

authorHOUSE®

AuthorHouse™ UK
1663 Liberty Drive
Bloomington, IN 47403 USA
www.authorhouse.co.uk
Phone: UK TFN: 0800 0148641 (Toll Free inside the UK)
UK Local: (02) 0369 56322 (+44 20 3695 6322 from outside the UK)

© 2023 Hugh Alexander. All rights reserved.

No part of this book may be reproduced, stored in a retrieval system, or transmitted by any means without the written permission of the author.

Published by AuthorHouse 07/04/2023

ISBN: 979-8-8230-8330-0 (sc)
ISBN: 979-8-8230-8331-7 (hc)
ISBN: 979-8-8230-8332-4 (e)

Print information available on the last page.

Any people depicted in stock imagery provided by Getty Images are models, and such images are being used for illustrative purposes only.
Certain stock imagery © Getty Images.

This book is printed on acid-free paper.

Because of the dynamic nature of the Internet, any web addresses or links contained in this book may have changed since publication and may no longer be valid. The views expressed in this work are solely those of the author and do not necessarily reflect the views of the publisher, and the publisher hereby disclaims any responsibility for them.

For my mother,
who invented the
'breakfast serial'

CONTENTS

Prologue ix

Chapter 1 Escape 1
Chapter 2 Morgan Field Associates 7
Chapter 3 Punster's Crack 10
Chapter 4 Yoruba 14
Chapter 5 Nest Egg 18
Chapter 6 Poste Restante 20
Chapter 7 External Internal 22
Chapter 8 Anomaly #1 25
Chapter 9 Stuart Andrews 30
Chapter 10 Anomaly #2 33
Chapter 11 The Library 44
Chapter 12 Anomaly #3 45
Chapter 13 Coffee Time 52
Chapter 14 Sunday Lunch 55
Chapter 15 Computer Centre—Client 57
Chapter 16 Why Hawks Kill Chickens 59
Chapter 17 Balerno Hill 61
Chapter 18 Computer Centre—Firm 65
Chapter 19 To London 75
Chapter 20 A Day in the Office 77
Chapter 21 London Meetings 79
Chapter 22 Chamonix-Mont-Blanc 83
Chapter 23 Mountaineering Council of Scotland 92

Chapter 24	Jerram	102
Chapter 25	La Traversée du Grépon	111
Chapter 26	Tré-le-Champ Wedding	115
Chapter 27	How a Hunter Obtained Money from His Friends, the Leopard, Goat, Bush Cat and Cock, and How He Got Out of Repaying Them	119
Chapter 28	Resting in Chamonix	123
Chapter 29	Victor de Clercq	129
Chapter 30	Vendetta	132
Chapter 31	Hydroglisse	133
Chapter 32	Igbinedion?	142
Chapter 33	Bivouac	147
Chapter 34	Stress	153
Chapter 35	Epiphany	155
Chapter 36	Intelligence	160
Chapter 37	Envers des Aiguilles	162
Chapter 38	Belaying	167
Chapter 39	Dinner for Three	169
Chapter 40	Reappraisal	172
Chapter 41	Dinner for Two	174
Chapter 42	Back to Work	177
Chapter 43	Sandwich Lunch	181
Chapter 44	Kalogiroi	184
Chapter 45	Final Touches	187
Chapter 46	A Completed Report	188
Chapter 47	Time to Leave	195
Chapter 48	Reparation	197

Epilogue 199

PROLOGUE

Never lend money to people
because if they cannot pay they
they will try to kill you or get rid
of you in some way, either by poison or
by setting bad Jujus for you.

> Southern Nigerian Folk Tale

Neither a borrower nor a lender be
For loan oft loses both itself and friend.

> *Hamlet*
> William Shakespeare

> **Yvonne Arnaud Art 2018—24th Summer Exhibition at the Mill Studio**
>
> # The Colours of Life
> ## J. F. Andrews
>
> **23 August—23 September**
> 10:00—17:00 daily
>
> A delightful exhibition of the works of local artist J. F. Andrews covering three distinct periods, from early favourites to her most recent creations.
>
> Jennifer Andrews was born in Edinburgh but has lived most of her life in the south. She painted throughout a successful financial career in big business. Now, married with two teenage children and living in Haslemere, Surrey, she is devoting her time more exclusively to her muse.
>
> Don't miss the chance to see this delightfully expressive collection.

"You are so full of it, Jenny!" one Jennifer said to another. "You make me sound like an artist."

"You *are* an artist, you numpty, which is why there is going to be an exhibition of your paintings and why people are going to come and look at them—and maybe pay quite large sums of money to take them away."

"I know, I know, but …"

x

"If I put out a flyer that said, 'Jennifer Wilson has spent her career as a boring accountant but has recently got quite good at her hobby, so do come along,' I wouldn't be doing my job very well, would I?"

Jennifer moved as if to slosh her large gin and tonic in her friend's direction but stayed her hand and raised the glass in tribute instead as they all laughed.

"You do a wonderful job, Jen," she said. "I don't know where I'd be without you."

Just under a year ago, Jennifer Wilson had come to a more formal arrangement about sales of her artwork with Jennifer Brown. This meant that Jenny B. had moved from being a helpful friend and advisor to someone who had a financial interest in every painting sold, every new commission gained (there had been two so far) and—as she had expanded things—in sales of numbered prints of some of the works. The website Jenny B. had set up was crucial to her marketing activities and was, of course, the main sales forum, although a rotating curated set of pictures was displayed on the premises of two local businesses now as well.

Jenny B. and her partner, Mark Behr, had been friends and near neighbours of Jennifer and Andrew Wilson for several years now. As they were coming to Jennifer and Andrew's for dinner, Jenny B. had brought the new flyers with her. Looking at them again, a thought struck her.

"Was it not a bit weird to change your name?" she asked.

Jennifer Andrews—or rather, J. F. Andrews—was the artist, but she was Jennifer Wilson for everything else.

"I can hardly even remember now, but no, I scarcely thought about it. I went from the start of the alphabet to the end of it, so I'm usually at the back of the queue now!" She looked towards Andrew with a smile. "I did suggest to 'his nibs' that he should take my name. I told him Andrew Andrews would make him sound like his own man."

Andrew gave her a sardonic smile.

"He wasn't keen."

"I was going to use both of our names for the children," Jenny B. replied, "but then it dawned on me that I couldn't send them to school as the Brown-Behr children."

"Perhaps we should have called Jack 'Bruno'," Mark suggested.

Unusually for a Saturday, Andrew had been working, on some big, new upgrade. As an IT architect for one of the large defence contractors, some antisocial hours were an *occasional* necessity. So, he had arrived back home scarcely before the neighbours had arrived and Jennifer had felt she may as well have had three guests. After he'd had a quick shower and got changed, though, he had made himself useful, lighting a few candles around the place and pouring her a drink. And he had made up for it in the morning by clearing up the bomb site of a kitchen almost single-handedly. After the best sex they'd had for some time, she had dozed a while and he had obviously been busy.

The things that have changed in the last twenty years! she thought. She hadn't even known Andrew back then. Now, here she was with a husband, two kids, and a dog, living in a lovely house. They had enough money to be much more comfortable than many and they were doing the things families do. She had reduced her work commitments to have enough time for the children—and she had time to paint. And people liked her paintings. But she could see the flaws in some of her early successes now and could see how she wanted to do better.

Standing in the kitchen, she looked at Andrew. Since she had received the letter and then had an initial short interview, she had been casting her mind back to a time when none of this was the case—to more than twenty years ago. So many changes. She kept remembering additional details—of how things had been and what had happened—and fitting them together. It seemed such a long time ago and yet seemed like only yesterday.

"Apparently, I 'reported clearly and cogently' at that time and 'made a good, authoritative witness'," she said.

Andrew realised her thoughts had turned again to the letter and her recent meeting.

"It's ironic," she continued, "because I was behaving anything other than 'clearly and cogently' back then."

She began to share her recollections: Sunday morning—lazy day, no real plans; David at his rugby tournament; Charlotte staying over with a friend. (A *girl*friend!) It did not all necessarily come out in chronological order, but—after pouring them both a fresh coffee—Andrew sat back and allowed himself to become immersed in the story.

CHAPTER

1

ESCAPE

Wednesday, 31 July 1996, 7:50 p.m.

At the end of his two-day exploratory visit to Cyprus, Irish envoy for the European Union Mr Kestler Heaslip is optimistic of progress.

Criticism continues after the solitary gold medal in Atlanta (thanks to Pinsent and Redgrave), is "Britain's feeblest Olympic campaign".

ANDREWS J 012D—the boarding card pointed her to a seat on the aisle. *That's fine*, she thought. She was feeling better now.

After charging around and being under such stress—feeling uncharacteristically panicky—she now relaxed. She paused and took a deep breath, let her head tilt back, and moved it gently from side to side, easing away the tension. Clearly, she may have overlooked something, but it seemed not. The arrangements she had made would not stand up to close scrutiny, she knew, but she hoped that they would be good enough not to need to. In any event, she could do no more. Her parameters had narrowed and all that remained now was for her to board the flight and be free.

This relieved feeling reminded her of her accountancy examinations. There was the stress of studying (or not studying—perhaps even more stressful) building up to a crescendo with the

Paper Chase

examination itself and then that wonderful feeling that there was nothing to be done except await the result. However well or badly she had studied in advance and performed on the day, there was no way to influence it now and hence no more stress.

In this frame of mind, she checked in her unfeasibly large rucksack and, unruffled now by the exhortations of the staff to hurry, as the flight had already had a final call, she made her way to the gate, the lightness of the hand baggage mirroring her mood.

Jennifer Andrews boarded the flight in this suddenly more relaxed frame of mind. The gin and tonic supplied soon after take-off added the final component to her relaxation. The penultimate one had been that the flight was only half full. The seat on her right was empty and the quiet businessman at the far end of the row of three appeared, like her, to prefer his own thoughts to cocktail chatter. Having smiled briefly at her in acknowledgment, he now gazed out over the wing unobtrusively.

Jenny knew that she could not relax and let her mind drift indefinitely. She had changed her plans but still had to deal with what was troubling and confusing her at work, so she must return to productive thought before long. Checking her watch—8:23 p.m.—she decided that 9:00 p.m. would be a useful marker for the end of her inactivity. Now she would think of nothing except the small tray which had arrived bearing a small roll, dainty pieces of sole meunière, cherry tomatoes, a quarter bottle of wine—everything in miniature form.

Some thirty minutes later, she was aware of a beautiful orange sunset, long after it would have been over at sea level. The sun seemed to be slipping away through the space between the sky and the land, spreading its dying, glorious fire the length of the vivid horizon. The calm landscape and the clear sky appeared subdued and sympathetic but not entirely part of the same scene, whilst delicate wisps of cloud hovered above, tinged with the warm colours, just out of harm's way.

From this reverie, she allowed her gaze to shorten and fall on her fellow traveller as he admired the scene outside. His profile could be discerned, but his head was turned away sufficiently for him to be unaware of her scrutiny.

He was a quietly handsome man, she thought, with a calm, wise aura. His features were well-defined, almost delicate, and yet there was a kind of brooding strength in them, matched by the way his dark-blue suit and white shirt were lit up by a loud tie, whose patterns reminded her of Inca drawings.

Suddenly, she thought that she had seen him somewhere before, or ... something seemed to register in her mind. She wondered idly who he was and where he was going.

(She said the man in the gabardine suit was a spy. I said be careful, his bow tie is really a camera.)

He turned and smiled at her as if in answer, as if he would offer the next line of the song. She was taken aback and was transfixed. His pale-blue eyes seemed to be imbued with extraordinary warmth and depth and they held her attention in a vertiginous grip. At the same time, these eyes had a penetrating quality. He seemed to look at her and through her, to see her whole life and know her intimately. She felt herself blush like a schoolgirl and hoped that it was not as obvious as it felt under the tranquil, godlike gaze of this man.

"Beautiful!" he said with just a trace of an accent, suggesting that English was not his first language. "I love the view from an aircraft."

French. He'd made a simple statement and seemed to know that he had her tacit agreement. She smiled and nodded and wondered what foolish romanticism had robbed her of the powers of speech and rational thought. She mentally shook herself and yet could not shake off the feeling that even this minor turmoil was on display to her companion.

"It is lovely," she offered, trying to recover some of her composure.

"I am not ashamed to say that I am a great admirer of beauty."

She was unsure whether to take this at face value.

"And I have been lucky enough to see a lot of it in my life so far."

"Do you travel a lot?" A rather banal question, she thought, but she had asked it now.

He seemed almost to laugh before checking himself. "I am sorry," he said. "I did not wish to offend you. It seems sometimes that I do nothing but travel, often by the slowest and most outdated methods. I spend a lot of my time in the mountains. When I am not off on an expedition elsewhere, I am usually acting as guide at home in the Haute-Savoie—in the Alps. I live near Chamonix. But you, too, are a lover of the mountains."

During this speech, her face had lit up, not just because she was indeed a lover of the mountains but because she knew where she had seen him before.

"Of course! You are Michel Louison! I was reading about you recently in one of the magazines."

"So you are a climber?"

"Yes, but not in the same way as—"

"Do you enjoy it, what you do?"

"Yes, but—"

"Then this is the main thing. No buts. Do it, enjoy it. No one is awarding points." He smiled again and gestured with his hand as if to apologise for his forceful interjection, for getting on his hobbyhorse. "I enjoy it."

His voice was distant, sonorous, reflective, and she seemed to see in his blue eyes many tall horizons.

"I always try not to lose that enjoyment, as some of my fellows have."

During the next half hour, she found out more about this intriguing and accomplished man and told him more about herself. The feeling that he already knew her well began to become less uncanny as some reality muddied the waters. She had blurted out the fact that she, too, was heading for Chamonix before she'd had time to think about it. He had asked her some perfectly innocent and reasonable questions, but they had seemed to her to be unreasonable probings.

Normally she would have been more candid and relaxed, but for such questions, she would have had to have time to think in advance, to construct a plausible and coherent fabrication, a web of deceit. *(Oh, what a tangled web we weave.)* She had not yet had that time and so had to be rather evasive. *(Why? "A well-earned break and a spot of climbing," would have sufficed.)* She had been so wrapped up in getting to this stage that she was losing the plot, she felt, and she had been chatting instead of thinking out how she would proceed from here.

He had sensed this screen of hesitation and had backed off. She could do no more than mourn the rift in their initial, easy rapport. He had nevertheless suggested that she should stay at his place, going on to explain to her open mouth that it was a kind of *gîte d'étape*, inhabited typically by thirty or more climbers, some of whom were his clients. There he had his offices as well as his private quarters.

"First officer, again. Just beginning our approach to Geneva. We'll be touching down in about fifteen minutes—that's just a fraction after 11:00 p.m. local time. That's 10:00 p.m. London time, if you care to change your watches. Conditions are calm and the temperature in Geneva is still eighteen degrees Celsius. It's really a rather pleasant evening. We'll be switching on the no-smoking signs in just a moment, so please make your way back to your seats for landing and enjoy the remainder of the flight."

The key points of this message were repeated in A-level French by an unseen female speaker, presumably a member of the cabin staff. Thankfully, Jenny thought, the smoking ban already applied to this flight, but she supposed old habits died hard.

The offer of accommodation—at least initial accommodation—had been left open, not pushed, but was influenced by onward travel. Jenny's idea had been to find some basic lodgings for the night and enquire about a rail or bus connection to Chamonix in

Paper Chase

the morning. Michel had a friend meeting him at the airport and it was only an hour by car to Chamonix.

There was really no decision to be made. In some ways, things were moving a bit too quickly for Jenny during this flight, but she was glad of the company and glad to be able to talk and distance herself from the past few days.

She was also childishly excited to be returning to Chamonix.

CHAPTER 2

MORGAN FIELD ASSOCIATES

> Wednesday, 31 July 1996, 07:25
>
> Prime Minister John Major and Taoiseach John Bruton had wide-ranging and positive discussions today. Both agreed useful progress had been made with the accord on rules and procedures and said they looked forward to getting down to substantive issues in renewed talks in September.

Cameron W. Field stared with open hostility at a passing traffic warden. An enforcer of the system was as worthy of his vitriol as the designer of it, he felt, on this chilly morning. In fact, it was a beautiful morning, with the clear air and blue skies which presaged another fine day, but there was a decided nip in the air in George Street at this hour. This slightly chilly beauty did not go unnoticed by Cameron, but he preferred to maintain his vitriolic temper for now *(nursing his wrath to keep it warm)*.

As a native of Edinburgh and a resident of the city, he felt that he was entitled to greater ease of parking than was the case. Even now, he walked past vacant bays, which would have been pounced on in seconds but for their residents-only designation. He would not have minded paying the exorbitant rate for the privilege of parking in such a space, but he could not do so, because he was a resident of a different zone. (This was not strictly true, as he would have minded very much, but he would probably have paid up in any case.) He already paid a small fortune each year to be permitted to park on the street outside his own house, if he was lucky enough to be able to locate a residents-only space—at least he would have had to consider doing so if his sumptuous apartment had not featured a large garage at street level. His wealth had some advantages.

Sometimes he found himself in a mood of this type—bitter and twisted, some of his colleagues said—but he didn't miss much. ("*I'm no' aye sleeping when my een are shut!*" his grandmother would have said.) Generally, he worked more efficiently on such days. He was aware that his secretary joked behind his back that he was either in a B & T mood or a G & T mood.

A tall and thin man of 44, Cameron William Field strode purposefully towards his office. He was dressed in a light-grey suit and—despite the season—a black woollen overcoat. Had he glanced in their direction, his black brogues would have gleamed back at him. As managing director of the general insurance division of Morgan Field Associates, one of the better-respected financial services companies still in private ownership, he felt that certain standards of appearance should be maintained. He invariably maintained them, both in himself and in his staff.

He had not always been so well disciplined in his manners or so serious about his work. When he had decided to change his slapdash ways and advance in the world of business, he had deliberately marked the transition by a change of name. Weathering the jibes of his more cynical colleagues, he had styled himself Cameron Field, which he felt to be more business-like and enigmatic than the mundane Bill Field he had always been before. He was still Bill (or even Billy) to his family and long-standing friends.

Cameron, which was his mother's maiden name, would have been his middle name, had his parents not had the wisdom to change the order. He was generally happier with the new name and its attendant persona, but he intensely disliked cheery clients abbreviating it to "Cam" and took every reasonable opportunity to reinforce all three syllables.

Turning into the entrance hall of the building, he spurned the lifts as usual, mentally bullet-pointing his day as he climbed the stairs to the fourth floor.

He did not, however, have a bullet point for the most important item of the day, since it was not known to him that he would shortly be arrested.

CHAPTER

3

PUNSTER'S CRACK

> Tuesday, 30 July 1996, 18:20
>
> At the Atlanta Olympics, Centennial Park reopens today after Saturday's bomb atrocity, which left two dead and well over 100 injured.
>
> Alan Shearer has become the most expensive footballer in the world, following his £15M transfer from Blackburn to Newcastle United.

"Wacko! Climb when ready!"

Simon knew, from this call, that he was now being safeguarded on the rope by his partner above him. He unfastened himself from his own belay and proceeded to recover the three pieces of gear it comprised: one "wire", an alloy wedge mounted on wire and fitted snugly into a tapering crack in the rock; one "friend", a camming device designed to apply an even, outward pressure upon loading so that it could be used as protection in even a completely parallel crack; one "sling", a simple nylon webbing sling looped over a spike of rock. Until now, these had been what fastened him, Simon "Wacko Jacko" Jackson, to the rock, together with his partner, who had been climbing above. Now, the call of "climb when ready" had confirmed that his partner, Mark, had created a similar belay some thirty metres above. Simon could climb up to join him and repeat the process. Always the methodical system of safety, in case of a fall, and always failing to safety. The new belay created and the partner safeguarded on the rope before the first belay is removed.

As soon as he had removed these three items and clipped them to his harness, Simon gave the next call: "Climbing!"

"OK!" came the reply—always the final confirmation from the leader.

As he heard the call of "climbing" and gave his affirmative response, Mark Waters was monitoring the tension on the twin ropes leading to his partner. Threaded through a friction device attached to his harness, the ropes could easily be locked by Mark to arrest the fall, should Simon slip. As Mark himself was attached to the rock by his belay, this was enough to ensure their safety.

Mark Waters—or "Watermark", as he was more commonly known—had been climbing like this for approaching ten years now, but he never tired of it. He enjoyed the feeling of moving over the rock, the process of reading the possibilities and solving the puzzle of how to make upward progress (in balance), the use of the equipment and the shapes and textures of the rock types. The camaraderie of the whole endeavour and the shared experience—all of these provided him ongoing satisfaction in the simple, natural activity of climbing. Throughout most of those ten years, Mark had known Wacko and had climbed with him frequently.

An odd mixture of genius and clown, dope and visionary, Simon could always be trusted to have an interesting and offbeat opinion, to be an excellent technician (albeit with occasional lapses of concentration) and generally to live up to his nickname, "Wacko Jacko". His namesake, Michael Jackson, was even more in the news these days—and usually for the wrong reasons now.

Simon had been known to have occasional short spells of remunerative employment, but mostly, he was a person of independent means. To the best of Mark's knowledge, this was due to a small family inheritance and a settlement following a much

Paper Chase

earlier injury at work, coupled with his simple and inexpensive lifestyle and frugal nature.

Mark, on the other hand, had always worked nine to five (and the rest), Monday to Friday, and had always been "Captain Sensible"—until recently. A month ago, he had been made redundant—out of the blue, as far as he was concerned. At least it meant he didn't have any *immediate* money worries. He spent most of his time, when at home, pursuing new employment, but he had often not been at home in the past month, as he had been spending quite a lot of time climbing.

Almost immediately, the slight tension on the ropes relaxed, meaning Simon had begun his ascent. Mark quickly took in the ropes to eliminate any slack, but did so without tugging, as Simon would be making delicate, balanced moves below. As the climb was not especially difficult, this upward progress was quite steady, with pauses only as Simon stopped to retrieve the safety equipment—the "running belays" which Mark had placed during his ascent. In a few minutes, Simon joined Mark on the small ledge, meaning that they had completed the penultimate pitch of this route. Simon would now continue to lead on and climb the final pitch. When he then brought Mark up to join him on top, the climb would be complete. In this case, the descent would be a simple scramble down from the summit to where they had started.

As they reached the top, the low cloud that had clung to the mountain all day suddenly cleared. They found themselves in hot sunshine with fine views over their mountain and the surrounding area. This particular mountain was called the Cobbler—or Ben Arthur, to give it its Sunday name—and this was the rocky and dramatic North Peak. Amazing to think that this was only a few miles north of the city of Glasgow. They could now clearly see the line of Ardgartan Arête leading up the right skyline of the South Peak, another "classic" line which they had in their sights. The route they had just completed was Punster's Crack and they had ticked off Recess Route earlier in the day.

The arête would have to wait, however, as it was already after seven o'clock and it would be nearer nine by the time they reached the village of Arrochar below. No restauration would be available by then. Fortunately, though, they had supplies in the van.

CHAPTER

4

YORUBA

Monday, 29 July 1996, 20:40

International counterterrorism measures will be boosted tomorrow as G7 leaders meet in Paris, following the Atlanta bomb and the TWA 800 crash.

Labour Party leader Mr Tony Blair is set to crack down on party dissidents amid signs that Labour could be facing a second summer of discontent.

"Mummy, I'm not sleepy and it's still light and how can I go to sleep if it is still daytime and I'm not sleepy?"

"Lie down now and I'll tell you a story. It might still be light, but it is late. If you listen to my story and try to imagine all the things I say to you, you will soon feel sleepy. I'll tell you the story of how our Yoruba people came to be on the earth and how Africa itself was made. Now, settle down, close your eyes and listen.

"In the beginning, there was only the sky above, water and marshland below.

"Olorun, the chief god, ruled the sky, and the goddess Olokun ruled what was below.

"Another god, Obatala, went to Olorun for permission to create dry land for all kinds of creatures to live on. He was given permission, so he asked for advice from Orunmila, who was the eldest son of Olorun and the god of prophecy.

"Orunmila told Obatala that he would need a gold chain long enough to reach below, a snail's shell filled with sand, a white hen, a black cat and a palm nut, all of which he was to carry in a bag. All the gods gave what gold they had and Orunmila supplied the other things.

"When everything was ready, Obatala hung the chain from a corner of the sky, put the bag over his shoulder and started to climb down. When he reached the end of the chain, he saw he still had some way to go. The chain did not reach!

"From above, Orunmila told him to pour out the sand from the snail's shell and also release the white hen. Obatala did as he was told. The hen, landing on the sand, immediately began scratching and scattering it. Wherever the sand settled, it formed dry land, the bigger piles becoming hills and the smaller piles valleys. Obatala jumped down on to a hill and named the place 'Ife'.

"The dry land now extended as far as he could see. He dug a hole and planted the palm nut and saw it grow to a mature tree in a flash. The mature palm tree dropped more palm nuts on the ground and each of these also grew immediately and repeated the process. Obatala built a hut and settled down, with the cat for company.

"Many months passed and Obatala grew bored with his routine. He decided to make beings like himself to keep him company. He dug into the sand and soon found clay, which he used to mould many figures like himself, but he grew tired and decided to take a break. He made wine from a nearby palm tree and drank bowl after bowl. Not realising he was drunk, Obatala returned to his task of creating the new beings and, because of his drunken condition, he made many imperfect figures. Without realising this, he called out to Olorun to breathe life into his beings.

"The next day he realised what he had done and swore never to drink again, but to take care of those who were deformed. And so he became protector of the deformed.

"The new people built huts, as Obatala had done, and soon Ife prospered and became a city. All the other gods were happy with what Obatala had done and visited the land often—all, that is, except for Olokun, the ruler of all below the sky. She had not been consulted by Obatala and grew angry that he had taken over so much of her kingdom. When Obatala returned to his home in the sky for a visit, Olokun summoned the great waves of her vast oceans and sent them surging across the land.

"She unleashed wave after wave, until much of the new land was underwater and many of the people were drowned. Those who had fled to the highest land pleaded with the god Eshu, who had been visiting, to return to the sky and report what was happening to them. Eshu demanded that sacrifices be made to Obatala and himself before he delivered the message. So, the people sacrificed some goats and Eshu returned to the sky.

"When Orunmila heard Eshu's message, he climbed down the golden chain to the earth and cast many spells which caused the flood waters to retreat and the dry African land to reappear for the people."

She was not sure how much of the tale her son had heard, but he had certainly not heard the end of it. With a smiling look at the beautiful, sleeping child, Adefolake Igbinedion walked softly from the room.

―⁓―

She went to bed not long afterwards with Efe. He had arrived, as expected, and let himself in unobtrusively while she had been telling the story. The next morning, when she woke, she was vaguely aware of him having left quietly maybe two hours ago. He always liked to be in very early to prepare for morning surgery and would probably have to go home first, she thought. As she got up, she saw that he had, as requested, left her the death certificate for Joachim Essilfie, the subject of the most recent claim. *Another of his patients gone,* she thought. *He'll have no earnings left.* She smiled to herself.

"Good morning, sleepyhead."

No verbal reply, but her thigh received a hug as she busied herself at the hob, preparing his favourite, shakshuka.

"Did you enjoy my story last night, Mayowa?"

"Yes. It was good."

"And did you hear it all? Do you remember it all?"

"Yes, I remember … maybe not all of the names, but I remember Efe."

"Efe?"

"Yes. Your 'special friend', Efe, same name as the world."

"Ah, Ife! You were paying attention. My special friend is Dr Efe, but the land in the story was called Ife. The land was just Ife, but the doctor is Dr Efemuaye Okonkwo. He's a very clever man. Do you remember all of the story?"

"Yes, I think so … but you can tell it to me again and I'll check."

"OK," she laughed. "Here's your breakfast."

CHAPTER 5

NEST EGG

Wednesday, 17 April 1996, 09:00

After four years of separation, the ten-year marriage of the Duke and Duchess of York ends in divorce.

Thirty-seven-year-old pop star Madonna, who once said she would advertise for a man to father her child, is pregnant and is said to be "deliriously happy".

He was under pressure for a variety of reasons. It did appear that he was under threat. There was all this Morgan family stuff and the new computer system issues. Would he ever get another job with his level of seniority at his age? It was easy to be confident when *in* a senior post, but how confident would he be as someone simply *aspiring* to that status?

Mentally, this was his justification for what he had done—for providing himself with a little "nest egg", authorised by "the other Cameron Field". Rental charges of £10,000 a month (for a leased office building, ostensibly) mounted up quite quickly and it was all done in such a way that it should not be noticed. By the time it was, he hoped to be long gone. He just needed a little something to top up his pension fund.

Through a "tweak" in the set-up of this account, these particular payments—and only these—now had different banking details associated with them: those of his numbered account with the newly-formed RCB Bank in Limassol, Cyprus. There were other overseas payments, so this should not raise much attention.

CHAPTER

6

POSTE RESTANTE

> Friday, 19 January 1996, 09:15
>
> The first MORI poll of 1996 shows Labour still comfortably ahead of the conservatives, with a showing of 55 per cent and a lead of 26 points.
>
> Daughter and sole heir of Elvis Presley, Lisa Marie Presley, has filed for divorce from the pop star Michael Jackson, ending a nineteen-month marriage.

Who would be a postman? She looked at the envelope again: "127/4 Walsingham Court". It just didn't exist. She seemed to spend half of her working life in these blocks and knew them well. There were always combinations of numbers coming up in addresses which did not actually occur in the building.

Here, in Walsingham Court, there was a rack of mailboxes on each floor to which she had to deliver post. Alongside each rack was a sort of mesh cage, which she supposed was originally for parcels. She always put the unallocated mail in one of the cages—the one which seemed to match the address most closely.

She mentally congratulated herself on this strategy, as the post was always claimed. The next time she visited, or at least within a few days, the cages were always empty.

Nearly finished here for today, she moved on down to the next floor.

On her way home from work, Ade Igbinedion popped into Walsingham Court and collected the unallocated mail from the various cages. Her tactic of using incorrect addresses within several of these housing blocks for her fictitious clients worked well.

CHAPTER

7

EXTERNAL INTERNAL

> Monday, 22 July 1996, 09:30
>
> Turkey's PM Erbakan has assured the self-declared Turkish Cypriot state of Ankara's support, amid signs of progress for the island.
>
> The Queen is concerned about security: photographers besieged the villa where the Princess of Wales was on holiday with her sons, buzzing it in helicopters.

"Morning, everyone."

There was a rather unenthusiastic grumble of "Good morning", with a hint of "Mr Field" appended by at least one person.

"This is Jennifer Andrews, our internal auditor—our *external* internal auditor—and she will be working with us over the next couple of weeks to give us our usual 'health check'. Obviously, this is an important part of our internal control system and of demonstrating our good governance generally, so I'm sure I can rely on you to give Jennifer every assistance in her work here. Katie, could you show Jennifer where she can base herself as we discussed? Thank you."

Cameron Field turned and left the assembled Edinburgh staff, pausing for a word with Jean Stovell, his PA, before disappearing into the smoked-glass calm of his office.

Based in London, Jenny's work took her all over the country, but she was pleased to be spending some time now in her native Edinburgh. She would have time to visit some old haunts, maybe, and catch up with old friends. Of course, Cameron Field was not particularly one of them. What little there had been between them that was extraneous to a strictly professional relationship was certainly in the past, and that's where it would stay. Also, she would have to visit her father sooner, rather than later.

"Morning, Jennifer. Katie Campbell."

Jenny shook the proffered hand of the young lady, who was very slim, very pretty, very elegant.

"Pleased to meet you, Katie," she said and instinctively knew that she meant it.

"It's this way."

Katie led the way back out through the main entrance doors, past the lift and through another double fire door.

"Toilets by the lift"—she gestured to the right with her slender hand, like an elegant air stewardess—"and staff room here." She mirrored the first gesture with her left hand. "'Staff room'. Listen to me. It's a bloody kitchen with a few seats in it!" she commented, so rapidly that Jenny could almost believe she had imagined it, before resuming her "professional guide" voice. "And this is the meeting room, which will be your office."

Katie opened the unlocked door, removing the key from the lock as she did so and handing it to Jenny as they walked in. It was a room with a table around which perhaps twelve people could be seated. There was a walk-in cupboard off it, which seemed to contain stationery items but not much else.

"You should have everything you need, but let me know if not. The photocopier, printer, fax machine and everything are in the main office. Just tell me if there's anything you need or if you have a query. You saw where my desk is—just on the right?"

"Yes. Thanks, Katie."

"If you don't mind me asking, what the bloody hell is an external internal auditor? It sounds like someone who doesn't

Paper Chase

know his arse from his elbow," she opined, adding quickly, "I'm sure you do, but!" in case of any offense.

Jenny smiled. "It's a bit of a crazy term," she said. "Basically, external auditors perform prescribed checks of accounts and solvency and so on, on behalf of the shareholders of the business, and internal auditors check on accounts, systems, processes, risks—internal control systems generally—on behalf of the board. What my team specialises in is providing the internal audit service as external contractors. So, it sounds paradoxical, but it saves the business from having to keep competent auditors on the payroll just to perform those internal control checks. Does that make sense?"

"Yes, I see. A bit like externalising your IT (which we don't) or facilities management or something?"

"Exactly. You've got it. So, effectively, I'm part of the team."

"Well, you're very welcome, teammate, and do let me know whenever you need something. There's always milk in there, by the way." She gestured through the wall towards the staff room. "Just use the one marked 'general'."

"OK, thanks again."

Jenny picked a seat and began to unload a few things from her bag as Katie left.

CHAPTER

8

ANOMALY #1

Tuesday, 23 July 1996, 11:00

"I've come across something I don't understand," Jenny said. "On the face of it, it looks as though obvious 'life' business is being allocated to the 'general' account. This all seems to be London-orientated business from …" She checked her notes.

"'Igbinedion' is the name I think you're looking for," put in Cameron Field, turning away from her to pull open a drawer of his filing cabinet.

Jenny had brought this to him, as the senior sponsor of the audit, just for a quick steer, as she was sure there was some plausible, if not perhaps completely textbook, explanation.

As he seemed to be familiar with the case, did he really need a file? Was he just stalling for time, or did he not want her to see his immediate reaction? Rather than survey the back of his head, Jenny glanced at the open drawer, which was just below eye level, as he withdrew a file marked "IGBIN". She froze for a second as he did so. The tab revealed on the file behind read "JERRAM".

Paper Chase

How to deal with this situation, thought Cameron Field. Several distinct strategies suggested themselves to him, but he was not yet sure which would be best to follow.

Damn Harold Hinton! he thought, even as he was vaguely thinking, *Damn Cameron Field.* Hinton had been his most senior account executive and—more often than not—the firm's principal source of new business. He had always been a real Morgan Field man and had been with the company for donkey's years—almost as long as Jean, his PA, who had started with Morgan Field as a junior administrator in 1960, when she was only 17. Harold had actually joined the firm a mere thirty years previously, in 1966, but that was still in the Dark Ages. Approaching 50 and finally realising that the Morgan Field opinion of Harold Hinton did not quite match up with his own opinion, Harold had resigned less than a year ago, moving to be a bigger fish in a smaller pond with a minor competitor.

It was somewhat ironic that—in a business governed by *uberrima fides*, or utmost good faith—Harold Hinton not only had a previous conviction for fraud but was also known to his golfing buddies as "Hooky Harry" because of his many questionable interpretations of the rules of golf. These two stains on his character were not very widely known. However, no sooner had he left and taken up his new role than Cameron Field had discovered this Igbin matter, where business that ought to have gone through the life division had been transacted through his general division. He had immediately acted in the matter, with righteous indignation.

"Harold? Can we arrange to meet? I need to speak to you about some irregularities I've discovered."

Harold had known this call had to come, but there had been nothing he could have done to prevent it. Two weeks into his new job and he was going to be distracted—and possibly discredited—by the past.

"I'm sure we can arrange that," he had said, attempting to use a light tone that did not reflect his recently changed mood.

Anomaly #1

Two hours later, they had been seated in a very quiet corner of a deserted lounge in the Caledonian Club, in Abercromby Place. This was Harold's club and the lounge was sumptuously appointed in red leather, including the fender seat around the blazing fire. It was very convenient for both men, but Cameron had declined any offer of refreshment.

"So, how much more of this sort of thing am I going to uncover, Harold?" Cameron had said.

"None. Absolutely none. There was one wrongly allocated account—"

"Over two years."

"One wrongly allocated account of which I became aware, but I didn't immediately correct it. It wouldn't have been reversed in time for the figures that month and then it had a bearing on the year-end figures." Harold's two raised palms forestalled another interruption. "I know it wasn't right, but I allowed it to continue in the short term to help our figures. You'll recall how much we were up against it at that time. But it was that one account only. From what you've said, you're fully aware of it, the Igbinedion account."

"OK but, apart from anything else, that means your own figures were boosted wrongly, as well as the company's. It's not just a question of irregular accounting and operating under the wrong supervisory regime. In taking any kind of bonus for those years, you've effectively defrauded the company as well."

"We can work that out and I can clearly reimburse anything in that category for those two years, but I obviously didn't want to draw attention to it at the time."

"Look, if that is all genuinely the case, then I'll try to keep a lid on it, but I can't make any promises."

Back in his own office, Cameron Field had considered the revenues over two years from this Igbinedion account and what effect their loss would have on his division's figures—including his staff's performance-related pay and his own bonus—and the current Morgan family negotiations.

He had allowed matters to rest there for a day, then a week. Now, after several months, he was well and truly implicated. And now his auditor—his ex- ... well, someone he had known for some time—was taking him to task.

"Look, Jenny, I'm already aware of this matter, as you'll gather. I'm afraid it's a legacy from my old chum, Mr Hinton. You're quite right. Somehow or other, he had ended up boosting his own figures—and kudos—by taking credit for new business that ought to have been passed straight away to the life division. He would still have got credit for the introduction but not in the same way. Instead, we have a sort of unofficial brokerage account with Synergy Life, where this business has been transacted on a redundant code, allied to the personal accident and travel business we have with them."

Is it just my imagination, Jenny thought, *or is he being a bit too chummy?*

"I have taken steps to regularise it all, but I have decided that what is already through will be left as an aberration. It would cause too much upheaval and frankly be far too visible to go back and correct it all *ab initio*. Also, a lot of politics is involved. So, given that you can now assure yourself that it's in hand and will not be a problem going forward, what I do not want is for any awkward issues to be raised by an audit report."

He paused and sent a smile across the desk which was devoid of any humour. Jenny stared for a moment, trying to maintain her composure.

"It may just be a mistake—I may have picked you up wrongly—but it almost sounds as though you're trying to put pressure on me to"—she hesitated, wanting to phrase this properly—"to suppress certain findings from my audit. You must be aware that I can't do that." She looked straight at him across the desk, assessing his reaction.

In the ensuing pause, her mind was already proposing ways in which this could be softened or disguised for everyone's sake—a coding error in a complex accounting environment, a different class of policy from the norm, perhaps a lack of familiarity with the new computer system—but she would not be bullied into covering up his division's misdemeanours.

CHAPTER

9

STUART ANDREWS

Wednesday, 24 July 1996, 20:15

Jenny parked the car on the lane and came into the garden through the tall, arched gate with the Sussex latch which breached the lovely old stone wall. She could easily have driven on a short distance and parked in the small yard near the back door, but she liked to come into her father's cottage this way.

She had never lived here. Her parents had moved not long after she'd first moved south as an ambitious 21-year-old in 1987. Ted had already been married, of course—Jenny was eight years younger. Her mum and dad had taken the opportunity to downsize a bit and mainly to move to a lovely rural setting, in Gifford. Her dad had been coming up to retirement then. Her parents had been thinking ahead, but they had not foreseen the late-diagnosed cancer from which her mum would die a year later at only 55. Her dad had been on his own for over seven years now. And then it had been Ted.

She walked on through lush greenery and followed the path to the right, towards the house. When she had last been here, the branches of the trees had appeared winter bare, but—when she'd looked closely—they had been covered in the beginnings of buds.

She had originally planned to visit at the weekend, but he was going to be away then, at a bowls competition in Aberfeldy. She was glad he had his bowling club for interest and exercise and camaraderie.

She was not going to get away with this any longer, as he had seen her approach through the conservatory and now came to the front door to greet her with a big hug.

"Jenny! Come away in. The kettle's hot."

"So, how do you like my new windows? Three thousand five hundred pounds' worth! I didn't want to leave them any longer, so I took a loan out to get them done now. I was speaking to Pete about it—you know Pete Wishart, from the bowling club—and he put me in touch with these J-Cash people."

Jenny stopped in her tracks. "J-Cash Services? As in Jerram? Oh, no!"

"What is it? It was all very easy and—"

"Dad, *I* could have loaned you that money—and charged a sensible rate of interest, if you liked—but there was no need to get mixed up with low life like this for the sake of three and a half thousand pounds."

"Oh, come on. I think you're being a bit unfair."

"They're basically criminals. I'd heard the name, but I've had to look into it for another reason. I've been in the library, in the old newspapers they have on microfiche. The tip of the iceberg that is in the public domain is already unsavoury, but it seems as though most of it is submerged. They've had frequent run-ins with the police and there are stories of people 'associated' with them being beaten up or even disappearing." The name had also been linked to numerous stories of drugs, money laundering and organised crime generally, but most had lacked any specific details. "I just can't believe you got mixed up with them."

"Well, see here, I won't have any trouble from them, because I'll make my repayments on time. Then, in a few months, that'll be the end of the matter. In the meantime, I have my new windows

Paper Chase

and that's an investment for the future—property improvement. I know you'll still say it would have been a bit cheaper with the bank, but Pete just made it seem so easy and it was a friend of his."

"Well, look, just make sure you do get your repayments in on time and don't have anything more to do with them. Let me know right away if anything else happens, like if they try to change the rules or something."

"All right, all right."

"I worry about you, Dad, and making decisions like this really doesn't help me not to."

"It'll be fine, especially since you've warned me now that I need to make sure I dot my 'i's and cross my 't's."

"Well, look, I'd better go. I don't want to be too late and I've still got some work to do. Enjoy the bowling! I'll arrange to drop in again before the end of the audit, but it won't be soon, as I'm off on leave after next week. Did I tell you?"

"No. I think I knew you had some holiday coming up some time."

"I'm going back to Chamonix. It'll be so good just to leave all this business stuff behind for a while and only have to worry about the weather and whether there's enough gas left to boil the kettle and what route to go for tomorrow. I'm really looking forward to it."

"Well, you be careful!"

"I will, Dad. I'll be back here the week beginning the nineteenth of August, so sometime that week, OK?"

"I'll look forward to it."

With a quick hug and a kiss, she was gone.

CHAPTER
10

ANOMALY #2

Thursday, 25 July 1996, 10:15

Jenny's head throbbed. Either these accounts were particularly convoluted, or else she was not thinking clearly. She was rather stuck at present. As ever, in auditing, it was not a question of checking the figures which were present, but those which were not—not adding up the numbers in front of you, but checking whether they were real and made sense. What was wrong? What was missing? Since she had discovered the Igbin anomaly, she was more on her guard than ever. She knew this report would be controversial—perhaps contested, certainly heavily scrutinised—and she wanted it to be right.

In her rather terse discussion with Cameron Field, he had hinted that he had set her up to get the Morgan Field external internal audit account as a personal favour—and not just that, but also that he had been influential with her director in having her very division set up to perform this kind of service. That was outrageous and fanciful, she thought. And what on earth did he have to do with Jerram? She was pretty sure he was not a Morgan Field client; she had seen all the lists. And now, her dad had got mixed up with Jerram's organisation. She wasn't concentrating.

She went for a walk. As was her habit when she got stuck, she stepped away from the problem. Don't the last three answers in

Paper Chase

yesterday's crossword always jump out at you when you pick it up again?

She considered locking the door of the room she was using for good measure, but there was nothing sensitive in what she was working on. She had, as always, closed up her files and her computer. The room was fine for her requirements, affording her a quiet place to work and also a place to have private meetings. The rest of the office was open plan, with the exception of Cameron Field's "goldfish bowl" and the room for which she now headed—the small kitchen/staff room next door. It was thankfully empty and she made herself a cup of tea. Actually, it wasn't even tea, but an infusion of ginger and herbs which had been a Christmas present from one of the kids, meaning that it was her sister-in-law's selection for her, really.

It was pleasant and soothing and she drifted. What must it be like to be widowed, with three young children, before the age of 40? Mel, her sister-in-law, had shown no signs of interest yet in other men. That time would come, Jenny supposed. For now, her whole focus was on the three lovely—*mostly* lovely—children.

She still felt the aching loss of her brother, but knew it must be worse for Mel. She also knew how hard it had hit her father. A bee knocked at the window and then flew off. Two days earlier, Tuesday, it had been a year and eight months since Ted had died—almost two years after being diagnosed, out of the blue, with motor neurone disease, an indiscriminate and heartless killer. He had died six years to the day after their mother, also on a Wednesday.

"'Hooky Harry'. That's what they call him."

She was dragged from her sad reverie by the arrival of a chattering group of broking staff members. Creatures of habit, they usually had a short tea break in the middle of the morning. "Cavatina" by Stanley Myers was what had been playing in her head, she now realised. It was the theme from *The Deer Hunter*. It always troubled her that it was written in 3/4 time but was usually played as though it was in 6/8.

"Yes, and do you know he's actually got a criminal prosecution for fraud?" Frank Green, a tall, mid-level broker, was warming to his audience now.

"Get right out of here!"

"No, he has—'Mr Holier-than-Thou', the fraudster! You know how the meters out on George Street are often jammed? They used to be more so. If you got one of them, you could stay on it for the rest of the day, free of charge, because they never used to check the times, just whether the meter was in credit. Well, some people used to jam them on purpose by sticking in a ring from a ring-pull can—when they used to come off, before they were attached—and then a two-pence piece. Apparently, Harold got to hear about this and tried it once—and he got caught. Because of the nature of what he'd done, the actual charge was fraud."

"Christ on a bike!" was the response from Katie Campbell. "He kept that quiet, but."

She had been very helpful to Jenny, who found some of her expressions at odds with her appearance. She was quite tall, very slim and pretty, as Jenny had noted before; very elegant and, at times, very crude.

The babble of conversation continued as Brian McGregor, drying the mug he had just washed, took a step or two towards her.

"I need to have a word, but I don't want it to be obvious. I can't afford for people to think I came to speak to you." He spoke quite naturally but also quite softly.

"Give me your name again," she said. She knew he was one of the senior men in IT and a sharp cookie, but she couldn't recall the name. "I have to select several people at random to interview. I'll make sure you're one of them. Then I'll have asked for you 'at random'."

This pleased him and he left, hanging up the tea towel en route.

Intriguing, she thought as she washed her own mug and put it in the cupboard beside her packet of "non-tea".

Paper Chase

"So I said, 'You might as well choose one-two-three-four-five-six,' and she said, 'Well, *that* wouldn't be very likely, would it?'"

Jenny didn't know this speaker, a fair-haired chap, but was vaguely aware that the group had switched to the subject of the lottery. Random.

As she was moving to leave, Jenny joined their conversation. "You know how you can increase your chances of winning more money on the lottery?"

"No. Surely it's all even. I mean …"

"Use larger numbers. You're right that you can't affect the chances of winning," she explained, "but if you use larger numbers, it's less likely that you would have to share a jackpot if you got it."

Katie was with her. "You mean because most people use birthdays as their numbers?"

"Yep! Lots of people do, anyway."

The others nodded in acknowledgment.

"You know," Jenny continued, "we used to have a lottery syndicate where I work in London, but it was a bit messy, as people had different shares. When it started, there were twenty-two members, then twenty-seven and eventually thirty, so it was all a bit complicated. So, one week, when it was a triple rollover, we agreed to put all the money in the kitty on as stakes. It was a hundred and forty-four pounds. Whatever we won would be shared, according to the formula, and from then on it would be thirty members and even shares."

"Makes sense," Katie said.

"Well, first of all, people wanted to choose their own numbers without checking."

"Meaning that, if two people picked the same numbers, you'd be betting against yourselves and wasting a pound," the fair-haired lad said. He was obviously the statistician among them.

"Exactly," Jenny replied. "But then there was a discussion about how likely a jackpot win was, and I said it was, in round figures, one in fourteen million. Except, we were putting on all the money, so we had one hundred and forty-four chances in fourteen million, or just a bit better than one in one hundred thousand. This sounded much better to some of them. 'Fourteen million down to less than a hundred thousand ... that's much better.' And then it was, 'I'd like to go to Jamaica,' and so on, so I felt I had to get it back into context. I told them 'Yes, so that means that, if we put one hundred forty-four lines on *every* week, the chances are that we should *win* the jackpot ... sometime in the next two thousand years!'"

That amused the others mildly.

"We don't even have that snowball's chance, because Mr Field doesn't approve," someone remonstrated.

"Nope. Gracie doesn't agree with the lottery," came another voice.

"Don't call Mr Field that," censured Katie. "He doesn't even have an S."

"I've heard he doesn't even have a *D*," retorted Frank Green, the comedian, to much laughter, although not much idea why.

Cameron Field returned to the office to find it almost deserted. Tea break! What did he pay these people for? He grunted a greeting at Jean in passing and seated himself at his desk. She followed him into the room, pointing to the desk in front of him.

"There's a note there for you from Mr Giles ... Morgan," she said, the surname almost an afterthought, "and there's the report you wanted to read before your two o'clock. Oh, and your agent in Cyprus has just called. There's been a cancellation for the week commencing the thirty-first of August."

"Good! Could you tell her I'll take that myself? I can check out how the work is going at number three while I'm there. Could you rejig anything I have on that week?"

Cameron Field had owned a small development of holiday villas in Girne (or Kyrenia) in the Turkish Republic of Northern

Paper Chase

Cyprus—a "state" recognised only by Turkey—for over two years now. At the time he'd bought it, it had been twenty years since the annexation of the north of the island by Turkey. Although it was officially still a complete aberration, there had been early signs on the ground that tensions were beginning to ease slightly. He had felt it was worth the risk. Now, under Ireland's presidency of the European Union, really positive advances were being made.

The properties were not quite as well used as he would have liked, but the utilisation rate did seem to compare well with other similar businesses. It was really all Turkish tourists at the moment, but all the signs were that it was set to become a more major holiday location for Britons, Germans and so on. He was in the habit of visiting twice a year—once in the summer and once in the winter—to keep a personal interest in what the agent was doing for him and because he found the area delightful and relaxing.

He had purchased the properties based on advice from "forward thinkers" in the business, but had not wanted to be as radical as to buy in Kurdistan, which they had assured him would be a major destination—the new Vietnam—with "Chemical Ali" and no-fly zones being quickly forgotten. He could already see things picking up in Northern Cyprus, though. He had not booked himself in yet this season purely because it had been so busy. The whole venture still turned a decent profit, even after paying huge fees to the agent and netting off a couple of free holidays for him each year. If he had been running things himself on the spot, it would have been a very good earner indeed.

He did not want to be there all the time, though, and did not really feel personally suited to running that sort of business. The agent knew the business and was good, which is why he paid her so much. And, because he paid highly for a good service, he could afford to be demanding. And he was demanding. That was the sort of business he did feel personally suited to, getting the best out of others.

Anomaly #2

Back in her room, Jenny found a large manila file had been left on her desk. This turned out to be the brief details of the life assurance policies sold by Ms Igbinedion and transacted through the incorrect channels. Rather than getting back to what she had been grappling with earlier, she had an initial look through this new material.

There were many policies, all "dread disease" (or "critical Illness", as it was also known), covering, as the name implied, most of the things people would be most worried about in terms of illness. This included cancer, heart failure, blindness, benign brain tumours and a whole range of other maladies, including HIV infection (in certain accidental circumstances) and—she couldn't help checking—motor neurone disease. The benefit payable, on suffering a qualifying illness, was typically £75,000 and sometimes £100,000. The application forms were included, together with proof of ID, usually including a copy of a passport. The applicants were mainly of West African or Caribbean origin, it seemed, and many of them seemed to share very similar addresses. It appeared that a large number of the applications came from one or another of what sounded like two blocks of flats.

As she continued to flick through the papers, something struck her. A man called Adebowale had a passport serial number which ended in 0310, which happened to be her date of birth, but she was sure she'd seen this number somewhere else before. She had always been one to see the "shape" and "internal rhymes" in numbers and it just struck her that she'd already seen this one. She knew she must be wrong, but wondered just how close it was, so she looked back through the file. She was just thinking that she was really wasting her time playing these games when she found it. She checked and found she had two identical passport numbers, one on the passport of the man called Adebowale and another on that of a woman called Agyepong. And yet, this Agyepong passport was not one she recalled having seen before.

Suddenly feeling uncomfortably warm in the room, she did a little more searching and found the original passport on which

Paper Chase

she had seen the number. She now had three different passports with different names, photographs and dates of birth, but with the same passport number. She stared for a few moments longer and then went out, locking the door behind her.

Moving through to the main, open-plan office, she located John Wade, the office manager, at his desk.

"OK, John, sorry to disturb you, but something's come up. I need all of the files for business placed with Synergy Life to be moved into my room."

John Wade's mouth started to open, but he looked at the expression on the face of Jennifer Andrews and wisely closed it again.

"I'll also need all of the accounting information for those cases from the start of the 1993/94 financial year copied on to one or more disks and also brought to me. I need all of that by five thirty this afternoon, please. It shouldn't be for long, but it is urgent. Also, if there is any communication from *anyone* on or in connection with one of those cases, I need to be informed about it immediately, and there should be no outward communication unless it's something of a routine nature that I have *specifically* authorised in advance. Again, that's only for now, but it's very important. Is that clear?" A small inclination of his head was enough for her purposes. "Thank you."

Back at her desk again, in the lull before she began to analyse the material she already had in more detail, she called her friend Simon from Leicester.

"Simon, hi. You know how you have certain talents with computers, which you've used on occasions and of which I don't entirely approve?"

"Yes…"

"Could you just see if you can find out anything about a woman called 'Igbinedion'?" She tested her recollection of the NATO phonetic alphabet by spelling the name out. "It might just be useful to have any background you can immediately discover.

Anomaly #2

I don't think there will be too many of them in the phone book. She's probably London based or nearby."

She didn't like it when one anomaly led to another. She was required to be "professionally sceptical" in order to perform her work.

"Hang on," she added. "First name 'Adefolake'." She thought she had better spell that one too.

"Jenny, you know this is nothing clever or secretive, really. It's called the *in-ter-net*, and there's just loads of information that's publicly available."

"But you've been able to find out things that are not publicly available at times too, though, haven't you?"

"I may have come across the odd nugget, due to the vagaries of computer coding protocols. Some of those guys are as daft as a biscuit, you know."

Always his idiosyncratic similes, she thought. On one classic occasion, he had accused someone of being as deaf as a bat.

"I also make a pretty fair mystery shopper, calling up at random."

"Well, just don't do anything dodgy. Don't get into any trouble. But let me know if you find anything out, OK?" She knew he was likely to have time to pursue a few enquiries, as he did not work for a living. She also knew that, if he did make a *faux pas*, it would not be traced back to her—well, she hoped not. No, of course not.

At random, she thought. *Like the numbers in the lottery. Like whether you contracted motor neurone disease or not. Like the inevitable risks you choose to take when you go to the mountains—fortunate that you are able to. Like the way your actions there are perceived. (Alison Hargreaves had died on K2 last August with a number of others—"summit fever", some said, while others said "suicidal". A storm in the media as well as on the mountain. One week earlier, Paul Nunn had been killed in the same area in a genuinely random incidence of icefall—the current chairman of the British Mountaineering Club and a giant of mountaineering, yet the story had warranted only a small paragraph in an inside page.) Random*

Paper Chase

like whether you happened to spot that two passport numbers are the same. So get on and do something about it, then, she finally chastised herself, snapping out of her reverie once more.

Within an hour, she had a list of all known clients from the Igbinedion connection, based on the details in the manila file. Within that list were three separate passport numbers which occurred more than once, usually three or four times. This suggested that there were at least ten or twelve bogus policies. She had a fraud on her hands. Many of the applications were completed in the same hand, with only the names, dates, signatures and perhaps a few notes appearing different. There was nothing wrong with that on the face of it. Earlier in her career, she herself had been expected (if not required) to be the one to deal with certain types of paperwork by clients who saw clerical work as something for the experts. On occasion, this had included being given a company cheque book for her to write out a cheque for her own fees.

So, there may be some regulatory breach, in terms of the procedures required in the sales of life assurance products, but not one of which she was presently aware. She would check, but that was secondary. Meanwhile, she wanted to know how many of the files on her left—half of the table was now covered with these individual cases, one row per passport number, while the others were in a single bundle to her right—had already become the subject of claims.

Her list included names, dates of birth, the dates of sale of policies, methods of identification, sums assured and comments. She added a column before the comments one labelled "Claim?" to which the date of any claim would be added when known.

Within another hour, the additional files and particulars had begun to arrive, brought in by John Wade and his helpers. She had to make use of the remainder of the large table and the window ledges in an ad hoc filing system.

Anomaly #2

Simon spent the rest of the morning and half of the afternoon on this enquiry before setting off to drive to Chichester to visit his friend Mark. He arrived in good time for them to go out and enjoy a fine curry. The only fault with it, from Simon's point of view, was that it cost twice as much as the equivalent in Leicester would have done.

CHAPTER 11

THE LIBRARY

Thursday, 25 July 1996, 16:30

Mayowa Igbinedion was a determined young man. The story of Obatala and how he had created not Efe (the doctor) but Ife (the world) had been running through his head again and again, but there were several details he could not remember. He did not want to admit this to his mother, which was why he had a look in her bookshelf when no one was around.

He did not think it was a secret place, just a bookshelf, but it was in her bedroom and he did have to stand on a chair to look in it properly. This was only because it was very small—smaller than a TV, he thought. It was just three narrow shelves with a decorative surround hung on the wall. It was at about the height of your head if you were a grown-up but much higher if you were only 8.

He was looking for something about Ife, Obatala (or any of the other gods), Yoruba, creation or anything about the story, but all of the books were about other things. He could find only two—both so slim he almost did not see them—which seemed to have any chance of containing his story. One was called *Igbo and Ibibio-Efik Folk Tales* and the other was called *Folk Stories from Southern Nigeria*. Thinking that the bookshelf must be like a library, Mayowa decided that he would borrow these two books for a short time. One of them must contain his story, he was sure.

CHAPTER

12

ANOMALY #3

Friday, 26 July 1996, 14:30

"Come in!" Jenny said.

Brian McGregor did so and turned to close the door behind him. He was a bit more smartly attired than most IT project managers she had come across and was certainly a few years older than her. Most of them still were.

One of the ... things (*advantage or disadvantage? varies*) about being an auditor, she mused, was that it was rather like life in the fast lane. You came into a large, complex organisation and you had to be sufficiently friendly to get under the skin of things very quickly yet sufficiently aloof to remain independent. You had to form an opinion as to what was going on. You always had to do a solid enough job and be nobody's fool, but there were some jobs which were dealt with much more thoroughly than others. You just couldn't afford to apply exactly the same rigour to each case, but—if you turned over a stone or two and found some things which were surprising or suspicious or just insufficiently explained—you certainly turned over a few more stones until you had got the full measure of what was what. The outcome was that, if you had first-class credentials and could get a prime slot with one of the world's "big six" accountancy firms in the first place, you whizzed around doing good work and constructing

Paper Chase

both an impressive CV and a very useful suitcase full of practical experience to go with it before you were 30, which Jenny would be very soon. That was quite a landmark age, according to most of her friends. For her own part, she did not set much sway by ages and random anniversaries based on how many fingers our species has.

She snapped out of it and focussed her attention on Brian.

"Brian, thank you very much for coming to see me."

He looked worried.

"I just need to ask you a few questions and it's nothing sinister. I can assure you that your selection was entirely random." She actually winked.

Brian seated himself around the end of the large table from her in the seat she had left drawn out for that purpose. They were, therefore, neither awkwardly side by side nor confrontationally opposite one another.

"Look, obviously, I do have a few standard questions to ask you," she said, "but why don't you go first. What is it you'd like to speak about?"

"I just wasn't really sure where to go with this," he began. "You know, sometimes you go through the proper channels—play it with a straight bat—and then it seems that it's gone wrong and so you question ... well, what is the right move?"

"OK, what sort of area are we talking about here?"

"Right, here it is in a nutshell. You know we've got a fairly new computer system in place?"

She inclined her head slightly, encouraging him to continue.

"Well, everyone is set up with a unique PIN—personal identification number—on the system, and then the appropriate privileges can be attached to each PIN, dependent on the nature of the role. Some time ago—about three months ago—I found an anomaly. It was one of the guys in the main office, a broker. You may have met him. Frank Green? But that doesn't matter. The thing was that, on his account, the normal access privilege controls couldn't be put in place effectively. The best advice I could get from the suppliers was to delete his PIN and set him up again, effectively as a new employee. So, I did that, except I couldn't immediately sort out how to delete the redundant PIN."

Jenny followed this in engaged silence, wondering where it was going.

"In the meantime, the replaced PIN continued to be active and no kind of warning arose to say that anything out of the ordinary had happened in the system—neither about the lack of privilege control nor about the substitution of the account." He seemed to expect a reaction but continued when he got none. "Now, bearing in mind that these IDs are supposed to be both unique and permanent, and bearing in mind that part of the set-up process is that you have to apply the appropriate privileges (and no one has *no* restrictions), I expected some kind of heads-up report to be raised, but there was nothing. Eventually, we worked out how to delete, or at least permanently incapacitate, the old PIN for Frank. You can't really delete stuff, because obviously the system is intended to keep a record of who did what when in perpetuity, or at least for as long as the archive records are set for whatever kind of area it is. Detail, OK."

He raised a self-heckling hand and checked himself for straying from the main narrative.

"Anyway, the main thing was, it was a bit of a worry. I reported it to Dennis—Dennis Wardlaw, my boss, the head of IT, not sure if you've met him yet—and also within the user group. You know how these things work," he said, by way of another aside. "At least half of the development requirement comes from existing users as a group, rather from the suppliers centrally. So, the user groups are important, as they give the suppliers the additional knowledge required to improve the product, and everyone can Bismarck the benefits."

"Bismarck?" Jenny raised an eyebrow at this unexplained term, even though it was within the context of an aside.

"Yes, you know. He said, 'I don't want to learn from *my* mistakes; I want to learn from the mistakes of *others*.' Anyway,

Paper Chase

I thought no more about it until I happened to come across something, just by accident, which showed that the extra PIN for Frank Green was still inactive but that a new one had been set up."

Now, he had her attention.

"I couldn't find out for sure, for fear of raising suspicion, but it seemed to have been set up six days after I had raised my concerns about the loophole in the system. I really wasn't sure what else to do about it, so I thought I'd take the chance and raise it with you when you were looking into systems of governance and internal control in your audit."

If she had more people like this, Jenny thought, her life would be much easier. She said, "So, we have an extra PIN set up, apparently just after you raised the anomaly."

"Yes, that's it."

"And has it been used for anything, or don't you know?"

"It hasn't been used at all on the system, as far as I'm aware. Actually," he corrected himself, "I'm not sure if I really checked."

"I think I'll be able to see what's been put through on each profile in the accounts, now that I'm on notice," Jenny said, thinking ahead.

"The real worry is that it's out there. Unless it's a coincidence, which I really don't believe, someone has created it on purpose. Sorry to be so cloak and dagger about it, but do you see why I'm concerned?"

"Someone—do you know who? Could you tell in whose name the new 'extra' ID was?"

"Well, that's the thing. It was in Mr Field's name."

Prompted by the meeting with Brian McGregor, Jenny managed to call up brief details of all of the PINs for all of the identities in the branch and the numbers appeared to tally with her record of the establishment numbers. Then she noticed the duplicate for Frank Green, now "closed", but no duplicate for Cameron

Anomaly #3

Field. In fact, there was no Cameron Field at all. That was why the establishment figure tallied—one missing, one extra. It dawned on her that Field would not be recorded on the system at branch level, but at a higher level in the organisational structure, yet he was shown on the less formal establishment record, presumably just because he was based there. She would need the head office background material, which would not normally be provided for her until she came to audit the top tier of the company, after all of the individual branches had been concluded.

Cameron Field was also operating at branch level, though. She found another way to locate some data, effectively a view of recent transactions by active ID. There were clearly reams and reams of this stuff, but she could not find a way to reorder the listing on her screen. She could refine the query to a single operator but did not have a reference for Field. So, she trawled through the pages of data, eventually finding an item in his name. The easiest way to do this was the old-fashioned way, she thought, opening her pad and copying all the details for that line. Two on-screen pages later, she found another Field entry and repeated the procedure. For most of his entries, there was much less information—they just identified a transaction without providing additional detail. She presumed these were operations at the higher level and the others, with full detail, concerned the branch.

After about forty minutes of this tedious, mechanical activity, just gathering data and making no effort to interpret it, she sat back and reviewed her findings, which amounted to one A4 page.

And there it was! All of the lines on her pad had the operator's name shown as "FIELD C" and then a reference. The third-to-last entry on the sheet, however, said "FIELD CW" and had a different reference from all of the rest. Obviously, this was only an oblique look at things and she would need the higher-level material to check this properly, but this backed up what Brian had told her. She would have to get the head office files early to bottom this out. Meanwhile, on a hunch, she went back to the screen and

Paper Chase

checked the transactions exactly one month earlier than this one. As she had suspected, there was an identical one there.

Checking her watch, she noticed it was approaching five o'clock—on a Friday afternoon. It would be a struggle to make the arrangements required to get these extra details now. So, she made a cryptic note to herself in her diary for Monday morning. She was done for today and had plans for the weekend. She would not think any more about any of this stuff until arriving back here on Monday morning—not if she could help it.

Now, she was going to the gym, through the reciprocal arrangement made with the hotel. She was not going home this weekend, as she had to be back in London midweek. (*Does it always have to be midweek?* she thought.) She had not been to the gym all week and was feeling the need for exercise. She resolved to fit in at least a couple of short sessions next week. It was not so practical to play badminton when away on these assignments, but there was nothing to stop her keeping fit in other ways.

Tomorrow, she would visit Alien Rock. She had never been there before, but it had opened a couple of years previously as Edinburgh's first dedicated indoor climbing centre. She could certainly use a bit of practice before her holiday, so she would head down to the waterfront at Newhaven in the morning. In the afternoon, she had some work to do to keep her department ticking over properly, nothing to do with Morgan Field. She had arranged to meet an old friend for lunch on Sunday.

On Monday, she would return to this matter. She had always been quite good at compartmentalising things in this way, she felt, to maintain her focus (and preserve her sanity). She sometimes felt guilty about doing this—for example, if what she was shutting out was how her father was getting on. When Ted had been ill and getting worse, she would visit and try to be upbeat, genuinely caring, of course, and genuinely admiring how positive he was in his actions and attitudes, despite his steadily increasing incapacity. Afterwards, though, she would go off and focus on other things—leaving his plight behind for the

Anomaly #3

moment—including mountaineering, which she could do and he could not and yet which risked the very privileges that she still had but that were now denied him.

She was contradicting herself. This was not compartmentalisation. She was out of here and more than ready for some simple, physical challenges in the gym.

CHAPTER 13

COFFEE TIME

Friday, 26 July 1996, 18:05

Cameron Field pressed the black button added to the consul of his Jaguar and the grille began to slide up. Slowing as he rounded the corner, he scarcely had to hesitate before pulling the car into his large ground-floor garage. No action was required on his part to close it again—the grille came back down automatically as soon as the ground beneath it was clear of obstruction. He rarely bothered to lock the car, in view of the quality of the garage security and of course the whole property was convincingly alarmed.

He retrieved his slim brief case and his coat from the back seat and unhooked his jacket from the peg behind the driver's seat. Then he crossed to the secure mailbox next to the personal entry system (or front door, as it may otherwise have been called) and collected the scanned items from the dispersal tray below it before mounting the sixteen steps which allowed him to enter the property's main level. Once inside, he dropped the outer garments on the lower part of the next staircase and walked through the end of the open-plan dining room, where he deposited his brief case and the letters on a Chippendale side table. It actually opened into a circular card table but had been a semicircular side table throughout most of his ownership.

Coffee Time

Walking straight through to the kitchen, he flicked a single switch on possibly his favourite machine—a teasmade, some may have called it, but it was actually a rather upmarket and authentic coffee maker by Krups. While the machine performed its magic, he went back to deal with the post. As usual, around half of it was dropped straight into the wastepaper bin, which sat to the left of the side table for this purpose. The remainder he divided into two roughly equal parts, laying aside the four to which he intended to give any attention. The others—only three, actually—he slit open, one after another, with his olive-wood-and-silver letter opener. He then proceeded to mix or dispose of the contents with practised ease.

These were the items of junk mail, from Barclaycard and others, that he had not dropped in the bin in the first cut, because experience told him they would contain business reply envelopes. Since these envelopes were just printed stationery at the point of issue and cost the senders more only when they were redeemed as postage-paid items, he would remove anything bearing his name or some other reference to him and stuff the remainder into one envelope or another. Thus, Barclaycard would receive holiday brochures, American Express perhaps some Barclaycard leaflets and the time-share people special offers of DIY tools. If he felt the envelopes were not full enough, he would add any other unattributable rubbish from the bin, often including the original window envelopes, suitably folded. If a reply envelope appeared to be too full for its meagre gum to hold shut, he would add Sellotape to ensure the appropriate postal charge applied and the junk reached its intended mark. Only in this way, he thought, would these idiots ever get the idea that it was not pleasant to receive junk mail.

The coffee was now ready and he took a cup to his favourite chair, together with the four genuine letters, already slit open. There were three routine bills and a bank statement. He glanced at the latter, which seemed to contain no surprises but at least one ongoing annoyance. His monthly salary, he knew, was £6,493 (the

Paper Chase

annual amount had to divide exactly by twelve, or the computer would melt) and yet he received only just over £3,500 of it, after tax, National Insurance, pension contributions and so on. Thank goodness there was also the monthly income of £10,000 from Gibraltar, whether or not he really approved of the source of it.

He set the distracting papers down and proceeded to savour his coffee.

CHAPTER

14

SUNDAY LUNCH

Sunday, 28 July 1996, 14:25

Jennifer Andrews enjoyed the last of what had really been a rather good fruit salad, served with ice cream instead of cream—and a wonderfully flavoursome real-vanilla ice cream at that. She had enjoyed her lunch, but it was a pity to be eating it alone, with only a few mildly interesting articles and some puzzles from yesterday's *Daily Telegraph* for company.

She had originally been due to meet an old friend from university, Rachel McLeod (Rachel Walker, she had been then). However, Rachel had telephoned the previous afternoon to call off. Apparently, the kids both had some nasty bug and she couldn't just dump them on her mother. So sorry. Next time.

Jenny had decided she would get out of town and have a nice lunch anyway, so she had come here to the Grey Horse Inn in Balerno. This was the place Rachel had suggested and she lived in Juniper Green, on the same side of town, and so should know if it was a good venue.

Putting her spoon down, Jenny pressed her palms together, the fingers turned towards her face, and stretched her poor forearms a little. Her arms were stiff from yesterday morning's exertions at what had been an excellent climbing wall, proving that she was in need of the practice. Her forearms were not the

Paper Chase

only bits that were stiff either. Perhaps she could get back there for another session sometime during next week. Annoyingly, she realised, "I Love to Love" by Tina Charles had been running through her head all morning. She tried to play some Mahler 4 to drive it out.

It had been good to get out of town again today—the visit to her father had been to the east; this time to the west—and she had enjoyed both the food and the friendly service. She had also enjoyed just relaxing, sipping a nice glass of Chenin blanc and reading the papers (OK, mainly doing the puzzles), but she knew that she had not had quite the same experience as the other tables—the couples out for a walk with dogs and the groups with lively discussions going on over roast dinners.

She drove back to the hotel by a circuitous route, Mozart playing in the car, enjoying the scenery and the bright, sunny day. She made one stop not long after leaving the Grey Horse, pulling over into the entrance to a field in the quiet lane. It was a lovely reverse-L-shaped composition—a stand of mature trees on the right leading up to a lovely old farmhouse, with the Pentland Hills in the background. Perched on the bonnet of the car, her feet on the front bumper and her drawing tablet on her knees, she did her best to capture it with her tin of Jaxell pastels. An hour later, she was actually quite pleased with the result.

CHAPTER 15

COMPUTER CENTRE—CLIENT

Monday, 29 July 1996, 12:00

"Yes, it was a definite flaw in the coding but not something we could immediately resolve, per se." Dennis Wardlaw leaned back in his chair and surveyed Jenny across a remarkably empty desk. "It's a very complex system and we can't exercise full control over it, or else we wouldn't have any backup from the suppliers when anything goes wrong or for routine system upgrades and so on. So, it just has to be added to the wish list and discussed within the user groups and so on, to try to get it higher up the prioritisation list for debugging by the suppliers. Meanwhile, we do have a very effective workaround. It was Brian McGregor who first spotted the problem. He brought it straight to me and we got it resolved pro tem."

Jenny had arranged to meet the head of IT in his office for two reasons. Firstly, she could more easily press for a more or less instant appointment if she came to him. Secondly, she had not had a reason to visit the computer centre before, despite it being only a short drive away at Sighthill, in the west of the city. Initially, she had retraced part of her route from the previous day.

She had taken a minor dislike to Mr Wardlaw already, although of course she tried not to show it. He seemed cooperative enough but a bit hapless—and annoying, in his mode of expression and

Paper Chase

tendency to justify things. He was probably good to his mother, she thought, if indeed he still had one. She would have put him in his early fifties and he was more than a little overweight. He was probably good at his job too. How would he react to a fast ball?

"What if I told you there was another duplicate ID and that it appears to be active, with regular payments being made under it?"

Jenny watched the reaction to this. Wardlaw looked very embarrassed, frightened, as if he was about to become very annoyed and as if he was about to burst into tears all at once. The shock of all of these conflicting emotions—or at least the appearance of them to Jenny—seemed to rob him of speech for a while.

When he did manage a response, it was to say, rather haltingly, "I'd be very disappointed to find out that our temporary solutions had failed to work fully, even though they could only ever be a second best, without being enforced within the actual system parameters."

As she drove back to the centre, Jenny thought rather bitterly to herself that she had had to rearrange two short interviews with members of staff in order to listen to platitudes like that from Wardlaw, meaning that most of this afternoon and Tuesday morning would now be taken up by these short, one-to-one meetings. They were important enough but easy and did not really help Jenny to get on with the trickier tasks she had to achieve. It had been important to have this discussion with Dennis Wardlaw as well, though, she felt. She just was not sure if it had really moved her much further forward.

CHAPTER 16

WHY HAWKS KILL CHICKENS

Many years ago, there was a young hen who was very pretty. A hawk saw her and at once fell for her beauty. There was a young cock who was also in love with the pretty hen, but she had eyes only for the hawk, who was very fast and strong.

And so, the hawk and the pretty hen were to be married. After the hawk had paid the bride price of the hen, married her and taken her to the Land of the Hawks, the desperate cock followed and crowed beautifully in his pain.

Hearing this and unable to resist the sweet crowing of the cock, the pretty hen left her husband's house and returned with the cock to the Land of Fowls.

Angry and feeling cheated, the hawk demanded the return of his dowry, as was the custom. The cock had no money and the pretty hen's parents had already spent the dowry, so neither could pay the hawk.

The hawk could not accept this and took the case to the king of animals, who decreed that the hawk could kill and eat any of the cock's children whenever and wherever he found them, in place of the repayment of his dowry. The king further decreed that any complaint from the cock would be ignored.

Paper Chase

And so, it has been the case, from that time long ago until now, that whenever a hawk sees a chicken he will swoop down and carry it off as partial repayment of his dowry and there is nothing that the cock can do about it. Any complaint he makes will be ignored by the king.

CHAPTER

17

BALERNO HILL

Tuesday, 30 July 1996, 15:15

Just before having to leave for her meeting with Dennis Wardlaw, Jenny had received the details of the dread-disease, or critical-illness (which now seemed to be the preferred term) policies. Specifically, this included those which had "matured" or become the subject of a claim. More than half of those on the left side of her table—the suspected fraudulent policies—had already come into this category and a total amount of more than £500,000 had been paid out as a result. It was too small a sample to be significant, as such, but this certainly appeared to be a much higher proportion than would have been expected from this number of cases if drawn at random. The ages at which the claims had been made did not seem to be an issue, as the average age for adult claimants in this area of cover was early fifties or even lower. However, it did seem as though the cases in her left-table sample had a shorter than average period between the inception of the policy and the onset of the ailment which gave rise to a claim.

This was as far as she had got with the data from Synergy Life—the company with which all of these Igbin policies had been placed—before she had had to go out to the Wardlaw meeting. Although they had been rather slower than she would have liked providing her with the basic data, Jenny was happy to concede

Paper Chase

that the person in the Synergy Life claims department with whom she had been dealing, a lady by the name of Catriona Rutherford, had been very helpful in illustrating the broader picture and what may or may not be significant. They did turn down a small proportion of the overall number of claims made against them—about 4 per cent—but in only about a quarter of those was the reason attempted fraud.

Now, just before her final short one-to-one interview of the day, this one with Katie Campbell, Jenny thought of another possible way to interrogate the Cameron Field transaction whose code was different from the others. Its record was lacking in detail, presumably because the transaction needed to be cleared at a higher level, as she had reasoned, so she was not very hopeful. Still, she tried all the same. Unexpectedly, she came up with a sort of floating comment. It was there, but she had nearly missed it. She would not have seen it if she had not been searching for anything at all, clutching at straws, in the first place. It was a bit like the kind of comment one may make within an Excel spreadsheet. She supposed that this really ought not to have been available at branch level but that it had slipped through as another vagary of the system. It said, "Lease of Unit 3, Balerno Hill Trading Estate; A/C 25920-748".

The reference 25920 appeared to be one which only Cameron Field used, or at least one not in use at branch level. She was able to see that it related to J-Cash Services, the Jerram short-period loan organisation. She had not even seen that one on the accounts listing before and had not believed it was a client of Morgan Field. In fact, it was definitely *not* on the client listing, so why had a client account been set up for it? This was not the procedure for a business contact who was a supplier, such as a landlord.

"Unit 3, Balerno Hill Trading Estate"—what was this mysterious location being used for? She had just been to Balerno. Where was the hill? Obviously somewhere else, despite having the same name. She got out her Edinburgh city plan with index (an old friend published by Bartholomew). Not listed. But how old was this map? She called the city council. No one could help. She called Royal Mail to find out the post code. No record of this location.

She looked at the few things scattered on her desk, as if some answer might be found there. The answer, if there was one, was surely to be found in her brain.

Cameron Field had a folder in his personal filing system which bore the name *Jerram*. Morgan Field Associates leased a building, apparently from J-Cash Services (Jerram's company), but she had no details, apart from the address. J-Cash Services was set up on the system as though it was a client but was not listed as such. Not only was the purpose of this leased building unclear, but the building itself seemed not to exist. The payee code was one which seemed to be specific to Field, or at least to senior management, rather than general branch affairs. From Friday's list, there were several recent transactions—all Field, of course. However, the code associated with this particular payee code, providing the financial system with the account to which to make payment, was different from the others on her list and was one she had never seen before—748. Significant? Hang on. Of course, this was also the transaction authorised by the other Cameron Field.

Before long, she had been able to unpick that code and trace its related banking details to a numbered account overseas (actually, in Cyprus). She felt the answer was yes—significant. She had thought Jerram was an Edinburgh hoodlum. Could he afford to be running overseas accounts just to cover his tracks—and avoid taxes, no doubt? And this was the man her father had got mixed up with! She couldn't quite believe it. But she had to focus. Did Cameron Field not have property in Cyprus? Was there some Cyprus connection between him and Jerram?

All these details were in strange backwaters of the financial system—areas you would not generally come across. For reporting purposes, their effect appeared to be rolled up into miscellaneous-type categories. Without the prompt she had had to commence this line of enquiry, she felt she would never have been aware of any of this. Like Alice, she felt this was all becoming "curiouser and curiouser".

The tap at the door was, of course, Katie. Jenny moved with her to the other end of the table, nearer to the door, which she had cleared again for the purpose of these meetings. She tried to use the table as an exemplar for her mind and clear it of the perplexing details she had just been considering, returning to lighter, more straightforward matters.

CHAPTER 18

COMPUTER CENTRE—FIRM

Tuesday, 30 July 1996, 17:25

Damn! Katie had gone and Jenny had been trying to pick up the threads, but now she realised that she had missed her diary note yesterday morning about requesting information. She had been working on the premise that she needed to see some more detailed figures and background but had effectively done nothing about it. She now had neither the time nor the inclination to go through the normal channels.

She could phone Mike Thomas at the computer centre in Glasgow. Her company's computer hub for the UK was located in Glasgow, perhaps only forty miles from the Morgan Field facility, which she had visited the day before. She knew Mike mainly from an in-house course on diversity and inclusion that they had attended together the previous year at the firm's training centre outside Bristol.

"Mike, hi. It's Jenny Andrews."

"Hi, Jenny, how are you?"

"Fine, thanks, but I need a little favour. Can you send me the full 1995 background report for audit 68423? Not branch stuff, just top level. It's a bit … unofficial, so I don't want to make a formal request at this stage, but it would speed things up."

"What are you like? I can't make an electronic copy without a bit of a palaver, which would be pretty visible, but I can put it on paper, if that's any good."

"That would be great. Can I pick it up? I'm in town already," she lied, "and will be finished up soon."

"Give me half an hour or so. After that, I may have to go, but I'll leave it for you in reception in a plain envelope. You can come in with your dark glasses on and your collar turned up."

"You've got it, Mike—mum's the word. And thanks. I owe you one."

She was joking, but she hoped he would be discreet. There were proper channels, after all, which she ought to have been following. Hopefully, the worst of the traffic would have subsided, so she could be there inside forty-five minutes if she left now. She could review the files tonight. The joys of having no social life to speak of, she thought. She couldn't be too late, as she had an early flight back to London in the morning.

Edinburgh and Glasgow being so close together encouraged cross-commuting, rather than the traffic being all in in the morning and out in the evening. Liverpool/Manchester and Southampton/Portsmouth were similar, she now knew, having had to conduct audits in most parts of the country.

The traffic was light, and she made good time. True to his word, Mike had done his bit. There was no one on the reception desk, but she could see the envelope with her name on it on the desk, half-tucked under the high counter, so she simply took it. *Great security,* she thought. But good—she'd sooner there was no record of her having been here. The envelope was slimmer than she had expected, but it contained a harder square, as well as papers. Good lad. He must have been able to put at least part of it on to a CD and it was the slim jewel case she was feeling. Without opening it, she folded the envelope in two and stuffed it into her bag.

Back in the car, she hurried homeward, thinking of how she would organise the evening. It would take two to three hours, she decided, to decipher the printouts properly, to make the necessary checks and notes and to summarise all of her findings in a concise report, the skeleton of which she had already prepared and saved, ready for the flesh to be added to the bones. This would not be a definitive report, just an interim. The traffic was lighter as she moved away from Glasgow's city centre and she speeded up a little to (more or less) catch the traffic lights. Then she noticed a police car on the left. Damn! She slowed a little and then heard two quick wails of the siren accompanied by flashing blue lights. Stupid! Stupid! She couldn't afford for this to happen now. *Why not?* she thought, but she had no real answer.

She slowed and pulled in to the side but didn't cut the engine. The police car followed her, taking too much for granted, she felt. She pulled away as soon as the driver was out of the car, scattering chippings in her wake. She had the element of surprise and quickly pulled away but with no intention of starting a chase. She took the first right just as the lights went to amber and then ducked into the car park of the pub on the left, nosing hastily into a convenient space near the rear entrance and cutting the engine before she had fully come to a stop. She snatched up her bag and entered the pub, not even bothering to lock her car.

As soon as she was inside, she felt concerned. She was making this up as she went along and did not feel she was making a good job of it.

(What am I doing? What was I thinking of? The car has licence plates, after all!)

She walked straight through the bar and out the front entrance on to the main road. A police car was turning into the car park to her left. A man of 50 or so was on the pavement. He was dressed in nondescript trousers, black shoes, white socks and a cheap 1970s bomber jacket, out of which a huge paunch protruded. He was beginning to cross the road towards the filling station and she went with him, matching his pace. (She nearly took his arm!) She followed him when he turned left but not when he entered

Paper Chase

the off-licence next to the filling station. She continued to the left, past a convenience store and several houses, to another pub.

She marched up to the bar and ordered a half pint of Stella, which was before her, dripping, in no time at all. She tried to calm herself as she surveyed her surroundings. This place was also a large, sprawling bar, with its own car park to the rear. It was busy enough to please the average landlord but quiet enough that she could count the patrons, if she felt so inclined. She had to get out of here but was wary of being caught on the street. *Steal a car,* she thought and then chastised herself for being both melodramatic and impractical. She had as much idea of how to break into a car as she had of how to run a bar. She had as much idea how to hot-wire one as to fly in the air.

Suddenly, she could almost hear the *ping!* in the air and feel the light bulb above her head. A dark-haired man (a salesman type, so full of himself, with too loud a voice) now on his way to the toilet had initially been fiddling incessantly with his keys on the bar, as if he'd wanted someone to ask him about them. She had been able to see that the key ring was from a Renault and had a handy remote-locking facility. He had left them on the bar, beside his change and a small notebook of some kind. Now, the audience for his last few larger-than-life tales had turned to address the man to his left. Jenny took a penultimate swig from her glass and set it down on the bar, positioning herself further to her left, hands on the bar, some way wider than her shoulders. This was a very macho position, she felt, but her right hand was near her glass, and her left was covering the unattended keys.

No one had paid any attention, so she drained her glass and set it down, raising her hand again in a gesture of "no, thanks, and farewell," to the barman, whose eyebrows were raised in her direction. He took the signal as only good telepathic, lip-reading bartenders can and turned away. She gathered in her splayed hands, pushed away from the bar, and headed for the car park. No one paid any attention, and no one yet missed the keys tucked in her left palm.

Like a weatherman trying and failing to be surreptitious with his little control button, she pressed the remote-locking device all the way down the car park. She was beginning to panic when finally a car she had almost passed suddenly lit up and all the doors clicked open. She got in as though it was fully paid for and drove off, turning left out of the car park and then right at the lights to continue her journey. As she passed, she could see the police car still in the car park opposite but hoped it might be some time before Loudmouth noticed the absence of his keys and even longer before he successfully filed a report.

She continued her journey as though the incident had never happened—except she was driving a stolen car, had left her own car behind (not even locked), and was being pursued by the police! To quell her rising panic, she tried to think of it as just another hired car, albeit one with an irritating paper coffee cup rolling around in the passenger footwell and magazines on the seat. Then she gradually tasked herself with considering what would/could/should happen next.

Jenny had always felt that sitting in the car, driving, was a good place to think. The only snag was that your good thoughts would not normally be recorded and so might be gone by the end of the journey. In this case, however, she held on to her conclusions and put her planning into practice.

Firstly, she pulled off the road towards central Edinburgh, heading for the airport to the west of the city. Taking a ticket from the machine at the entry gate, she parked in the short-term parking. She then fished a scarf out of her bag and, feeling like a character in a play, carefully wiped the steering wheel, gear lever, handbrake and indicator stalk. Then, chastising herself for the near omission, she also wiped the seat belt buckle. Before closing the door and wiping the handle, she tucked the wiped keys behind the sun visor. Replacing the scarf and slinging her bag over her

Paper Chase

shoulder, she walked around to the taxi rank and caught a cab towards the city centre. She directed the driver further north to Stockbridge and was dropped off near where her car had been parked. As the taxi headed off, she took out her mobile phone and dialled 999.

"Emergency. Which service, please?"

"Police."

"One moment, please."

"Police emergency. Can I help you?"

"Look, I'm not sure I should be calling this number, but I'm on my mobile and I'm not sure what other number to call."

"What is the problem, madam?"

"My car's been stolen."

"Was it taken from you, or have you just discovered it gone?"

"I've just come to get it and it's not here."

"One moment … where are you calling from, madam?"

"From Dean Park Street, Stockbridge."

"In Edinburgh."

"Yes."

"Do you have a pen?"

With good grace, Jenny thought, she was given the correct number to call. It rang for a long time, but eventually she was able to file an initial report of her "stolen" car. Having done so, she began to climb the hill again to George Street and her present place of employment, stopping at a late-opening corner shop to buy a small packet of self-sealing envelopes—no window—and a book of first-class stamps.

There seemed to be no one around at this hour and Jenny unlocked her room and let herself in, resisting the temptation to lock the door behind her. Once at her desk, she opened the envelopes and addressed one to the Glasgow pub—as well as she could remember—using a black Biro and what she believed to be completely characterless block letters. She used the same lettering to add the stolen car's registration number to the airport car park ticket and "E18" as the location within the car park.

Computer Centre—Firm

Then, retrieving her trusty scarf, she carefully wiped the ticket and tucked it into the envelope. She affixed a first-class stamp—self-adhesive, fortunately—and then wiped the whole envelope with the scarf and put it into her bag inside a folded sheet of plain paper.

She left the room and turned to lock the door but physically jumped as Katie came out of the main office, heading for the lifts.

"Oh, I thought you'd left. There were two police officers here looking for you. I don't know why. I told them you'd gone home."

"When was this?" Jenny wanted to know.

"Just a few minutes ago."

"I must just have gone out. I had left, but when I got to the car, it wasn't there."

"What?"

"It seems to have been stolen."

"Shite and abortion!" Katie sympathised. "Is that why …? No."

The question drifted off as she came up with her own answer. Too soon, so the police officers must have been after something else.

"Unless they towed your car away," Katie added as an afterthought.

They laughed, hoping it was a joke. Jenny, of course, knew that she must have been "wanted" for something else, but what? Surely not anything that happened in Glasgow. How had she transformed herself from a responsible businesswoman into some kind of fugitive?

They drifted into silence during the short lift journey, but it was broken by Katie after they reached the ground floor.

"I'd offer you a lift, but I'm on the bus myself."

"Thanks, anyway."

Katie headed down towards Princes Street, and Jenny went east on George Street, walking two blocks plus in the wrong direction before finding what she felt was a suitable post box. She fished in her bag and took out the folded sheet of paper, with the envelope inside it. She posted this, allowing the envelope to

Paper Chase

slip out while retaining the blank sheet. Rather than open her bag again, she crushed the paper up and tossed it into a wastepaper bin as she made her way back west and then north. She headed for the police station off Comely Bank, a little way further out of town than where she had parked her car, to formalise her report. As she neared the police station, walking along Fettes Avenue, she could see the towering central spire and huge east and west wings of Fettes College, which inhabited its own ample grounds at the end of the street. She could think of only two former pupils of Fettes. One was a girl called Sue Carmichael, who had beaten her in the semi-finals of a badminton tournament, and the other was the new young leader of the labour party, possibly the next prime minister, she thought. "Bambi" they called him, but he was making headway.

―⁂―

Having dealt with the formalities of the "theft" of her car—and having managed to visit a police station without being clapped in irons—Jenny walked back towards the centre. She had tried to call the hire company but could get no answer, so she had made a note to call in the morning. As she walked past where the car had been parked earlier, she tried to recall recovering it on her way to Glasgow. She could not remember anyone having been around, but she really had not been paying attention. She continued on the main road through Bohemian Stockbridge, over the Water of Leith and up into the Royal Circus. Aside from being a wanted criminal (she hoped that was a joke too), she was pleased to be back in Edinburgh. This was a real place—it was "in use"—but still, the architecture and layout of the New Town were magnificent. What a concept! The city had recently been made a UNESCO World Heritage Site for its architecture. She suddenly realised the Brandenburg Concertos had been playing in her head for a while, but she was not sure for how long. Specifically, it was the first movement of the second concerto. She stopped and then moved forward a little, then right a little, framing the view to advantage and then operating the camera in her brain. She studied the details of the elegant but sturdy Georgian architecture curving up the hill to her left; the stone wall and black iron railings bordering the gardens to her right; the gardens themselves—grass, paths, benches and most of all the beautiful trees. She would sketch this when she got back to her room. (She should have looked more closely at Fettes College—another time.)

She moved on. Doing a dog's leg out of the Royal Circus—there was no direct way—she gained Great King Street, the location of her hotel. She always stayed at the Howard Hotel when in Edinburgh. It was rather more grand than her normal selections, but the group was a client, so it was seen as reciprocal business, despite the substantial discount they received as regular users. She knew the arrangement was made more for her senior colleagues, many of whom had frequent visits to the capital for board meetings and the like (and who often then used Edinburgh as a base for travel further north, to sample the country delights of "huntin', shootin', 'n' fishin'"), but she was happy to ride on their coat-tails. It was a delightful hotel within very easy striking distance of the city centre.

Once back in her room, Jenny switched on the CD player and played the wonderful Sibelius 5—she rarely travelled without it. She put the kettle on to boil and then went for a quick shower, luxuriating in the well-appointed bathroom. Returning with one towel wrapped around her body and another forming a rough turban, she put a tea bag into a cup and switched the kettle on again before almost immediately changing her mind and switching it off. Instead, she reached into the minibar and enjoyed a glass of cold, fruity wine while she packed a few things for the morning. She booked a taxi. She had no time to faff around with public transport and there was no point even trying to get a replacement hire car now. She would arrange for one to be ready for her return from London when she called the hire company in the morning. She quickly sketched her image of the Royal Circus—just enough

Paper Chase

to fix the composition but with several zoomed-in details added around the outside. Like Ruskin's *The Stones of Venice,* she thought with a smile.

Finishing her drink, she picked up the plain envelope from Mike Thomas and turned it over in her hands but did not open it. She set her alarm for the morning and was asleep before ten o'clock.

CHAPTER
19

TO LONDON

Wednesday, 31 July 1996, 06:40

Jenny yawned as she flicked through the papers for the afternoon's MR, or monthly review meeting. It was regarded as good practice for all the heads of department to get together each month and compare notes. It was not *exactly* a three-line whip, but non-attendance was certainly frowned upon. Exactly how much she would say about the unusual aspects of her current assignment would depend upon this morning's meeting with her boss. That was another unknown quantity, at the moment. She bit her lip and glanced up. Seated (fortunately) at her gate in Edinburgh Airport, she expected the early morning flight to be called very soon.

The days of the Shuttle had gone now—no more just turning up and paying your £80 on the plane with a credit card. This run was still a little like a bus service, though, particularly when Jenny just had to make a quick call to her travel people to sort out reservations. So much time travelling, but she could use the time to read anything which was not sensitive, write notes and think, whether here, on the flight itself, or rattling in on the Piccadilly line from Heathrow to the City. She would soon be on holiday anyway—more travel, but of a very different sort. Much more pleasant. This time next week, she would be climbing in the Alps!

Paper Chase

She glanced at the printout of her diary for this week, for today in particular.

She really wasn't sure how the meeting with Mike would go. Mike Da'eth, her boss, generally gave her a lot of freedom. He was

	Wednesday, 31 July
07:00–08:10	Early flight EDI/LHR
09:30–11:00	Catch up at desk
11:30–12:00	1:1 MRD/JFA (his office)
12:30–13:30	Quick lunch with Julie E
14:00– 16:00	MR—Meeting Room 3

supportive but not inclined to micromanage. When he did want something done in a certain way or in a certain order of priority, she was generally happy to shrug her shoulders and fall in line. He was the boss. At their last meeting, however, they had got rather at loggerheads. For some reason, they had both dug in and failed to see eye to eye. That particular issue had now been resolved, but it still left something of a cloud. Actually, it had not been fully resolved—to some extent it had just "gone away". That made for even more uncertainty, which she could have done without.

Well, she thought as she walked forward to board her flight, she would find out how the land lay soon enough.

CHAPTER

20

A DAY IN THE OFFICE

Wednesday, 31 July 1996, 07:30

After completing his bullet-pointing of the day while ascending the stairs, Cameron Field let himself into his office and settled himself behind his large desk. There seemed to be no one else around, but he could not be sure. There were some other early birds on the team. Jean would be in at eight o'clock, bringing him the *Financial Times* and a cup of ordinary (but acceptable) coffee.

He had no appointments scheduled for the day, but he had a lot of work to get through. For some reason, though, his thoughts turned to Lilian, his wife, whom he had not seen since they had separated thirteen years ago. Five years older than him, she would be nearly 50 now. And more especially, he thought of his son, James. Born in 1976, he would be 20. From his wallet, he pulled out a small, square photograph. A tousled 4-year-old in little denim dungarees peeped around the garden shed towards the unseen camera, a cheeky, expectant smile playing on his lips.

He looked at the photograph and through it. Twenty! A young man. After a time—he had no idea how long—he pushed the photograph back into his wallet and forced himself back to regional representation plans and completing the medium-term financial strategy.

Paper Chase

Just before noon, it was something of a surprise when Jean asked if she could show in two detectives.

He consented and they proceeded to ask awkward questions about Jerram and his business affairs and about Field's association with him. They were also hinting at all sorts of financial improprieties as they gave a fairly poor, amateur-dramatics-type rendition of good cop, bad cop.

They asked if he would accompany them to the station to answer a few questions, which was slightly bizarre, as here they were asking questions already. However, he acceded, as he really did not want them hanging around here. Telling Jean he would be out for a while, he led them back through the main office and out.

Jean was speaking to Brian McGregor, who was there dealing with a network issue, as Cameron had left with the two detectives, and she noticed that Brian seemed to look at him oddly. She wondered if he knew one of the detectives. If so, it would certainly cause an eyebrow to raise. Brian, the poor soul, was bearing up well, in view of the business with his brother's suicide, which is what she had been speaking to him about. Just sympathising, really. She had only heard about it through her piano playing. She still did not think of herself as very much of a pianist, but she had acted as accompanist for the church choir for over three years now. She really was not involved with the church otherwise, but that was how she had heard.

No one else appeared to think it was odd that the boss should be going out, apparently for lunch, with these two rather casually dressed gentlemen. No doubt, they were prospective new clients.

CHAPTER
21

LONDON MEETINGS

Wednesday, 31 July 1996, 11:25

Jenny's desk had been quite quiet, considering the length of time she had been away, without too many messages and problems to attend to, from her own staff or otherwise. She had had time to do some preparation for the MR and, more urgently, for the meeting she was now heading towards. She would keep the details of the problems with her current assignment quite precise—brief and objective—letting her boss drill down for more detail if he wished to. They were unlikely to have any more time than the allotted thirty minutes. This was ridiculous, she thought, to be feeling nervous about a meeting with her boss. She had always got on well with him, despite his nickname. (He did have a doctorate and so, fairly obviously, was generally caricatured as Dr Death.) She reached his front office.

"Hi, Bryony. Is Mike free?"

"Oh, Jennifer, he's not here. Didn't you have a message? He's been called away to New York."

Bryony Matthews, Mike's PA and a very suave 40-year-old, was usually the epitome of efficiency, but Jenny was pretty sure there had been no message. In any event, the fact of the matter was that Mike was overseas and there would be no meeting this morning. There was a small element of relief, but that was just putting things off. She had been all ready to have this meeting and get things back on an even keel again. Besides, she now had to make up her own mind how candid to be, at this early stage, in this afternoon's meeting. Although she knew that these things happened and that Mike had quite a phenomenal workload, she could not help feeling somewhat slighted.

She got through the rest of the day with a fairly minimal report at the MR, hinting at areas of concern she was looking into rather than becoming too specific at this stage. At least she had had a lovely lunch with her friend Julie Eriksson. They had also bumped into Edith Adebayo in the street, a mutual friend—who was pregnant!

Jenny cleared out early, virtually as soon as the MR was over. It had been chaired by Roger, in Mike's absence, and he was not known for dragging these things out. She must look at the file from Mike Thomas tonight, she thought, assuming her flat had not flooded or burned down or something. She would be off again early in the morning and would benefit from the extra time to absorb anything she found there and perhaps be more ready to make further enquiries.

Catching the tube at Bank, she took the Central line to Bond Street and then the Jubilee line to Finchley Road, a journey she could do in her sleep. She then walked the short distance to her flat in Goldhurst Terrace. As she turned into the street, thinking of other things, she nearly froze when she saw a police car parked almost opposite her flat. There were two officers seated in the car, which was facing the other way, as the street was one way. This was not commonplace, but then again, the police were all over in London. This could not be anything to do with her.

Nevertheless, scarcely missing a beat, she cut right up the lane and made her way along until she could let herself into the small enclosed garden to the rear of the block, accessing the stairs from there. Fortunately, she always kept all the keys she was likely to need on a single ring.

No flood, no fire, but what was going on outside? There was a bundle of mail for her and four messages on the answering machine but nothing urgent. She made notes on a pad and then tore the sheet off and stuffed it into a pocket in her bag. Edging towards the window, she could still see the roof of the police car.

Ping! The light bulb flashed on above her head again—almost blinding her, she thought. Blindingly obvious, she thought. It came to her all at once, all aspects of it.

She was due off on leave at the weekend. She was back home now. There was no point in flying back up to Edinburgh tomorrow for two days' work, especially when she did not know how she would proceed or what her exact priorities would be. And especially when she would not complete the audit. Even before the problems she had encountered, she had had the week after her leave booked in to complete it. (Whose crazy idea had it been to zoom up and down the country like that anyway? Hers, she supposed, but it was crazy, when she came to think about it.) And her rucksack was packed ready for her trip to the Alps. Before she had left, she had packed up on a trial basis—thoroughly, including everything on her list—so that she could check that everything fitted into her new rucksack and weigh it with the spring balance she used to see how bad the excess baggage was likely to be. She had not had time to unpack it and put everything away and it was sitting there, like a big friend, in the bedroom.

All this came to her in a flash. All she had to do was get out of here and pay a few pounds to change the timing of her ticket to Geneva. She was pretty sure there was a late-evening flight, which she should still be able to catch, if it was not full. London thought she was in Edinburgh the rest of the week. She could make an excuse about London to Edinburgh and see them again after her leave. The car hire company was another call for the next morning. She had called them when she'd got into the office, but had been unable to get through at the time. Then it had slipped her mind, so there would be no hire car waiting for her. She just needed to get out of whatever was going on here and to relax for

Paper Chase

a bit—well, partly that, but also to review matters during rest time in the Alps and see where they went next. Better perspective.

She quickly changed into some casual, outdoor clothes and transferred all the papers she had been carrying and a few other necessaries from her travel case to a small carry-on rucksack, ensuring that her travel wallet was included, with passport, ticket and so on. She stuffed the post she had just collected and her handbag into the small rucksack as well.

Edging to the window again, she could see that the police car was gone. She glanced around the flat, but it had been in a fit state to be left unattended until now and she had not changed anything. She hefted the big rucksack. It really was a great piece of kit. A Lowe Alpine Alpamayo with a capacity of ninety litres. It had cost her nearly £150, but it just ate up her gear. Although now weighing thirty-five kilograms, it distributed the weight so well that it felt really comfortable. She pulled the small rucksack on in front of her like a papoose and locked her flat behind her.

The police car may have gone, but she left the property as she had come in, from the rear, and rejoined Goldhurst Terrace from the lane. The trip from Finchley Road to Green Park and then from Green Park to Heathrow was almost as familiar to her as her trip home from Bank.

After an uneventful journey to the airport, this plan still seemed a good one, especially when she arrived in time to change her ticket over and check in for the evening flight to Geneva. She scarcely even begrudged the admin fee.

"ANDREWS J 012D", it said on her boarding card, as she checked in the unfeasibly large rucksack.

CHAPTER 22

CHAMONIX-MONT-BLANC

jeudi, 1 août 1996, 07:15

Jenny woke quite early but feeling wonderfully relaxed and refreshed. She was alone in a bunkhouse-type room which would have slept twelve or more quite easily. It was at the far end of the lowest floor of the chalet, effectively the cellar level. She had not paid much attention last night but reviewed the layout this morning. There was a garage/workshop down here with space for a couple of cars, though none in evidence. There was enough of a store of foodstuffs to launch a small shop and loads of gear—boots, skis, helmets, ropes, you name it. She climbed the stairs to the main level. There were several doors to the rear side of the chalet (private bedrooms, study and the like, Jenny supposed), but the whole front part of the property was a huge open-plan room. There was a well-equipped kitchen area at one end behind a long counter with seating. At the other end was a great wooden table with long benches on all four sides. In the middle of the room was the largest stove Jenny had ever seen, with wood stored all around and under it in a kind of bund. The flue from the stove turned at right angles and ran along, below ceiling height, to the back of the property, where it disappeared upward. This flue was obviously used for casual drying purposes. A ramshackle collection of bookshelves was interestingly overflowing on the

Paper Chase

wall near the table end. Somehow, the place looked cosy, despite its pronounced feeling of space and possibility.

This floor was well above ground level, especially at the front, and a broad balcony ran around three sides under cover of the eaves. It was bright and airy, but she could see that the windows were heavily double shuttered for less amenable weather conditions. Although she had not seen it yet, she had been told that the whole attic was a bunkhouse for up to forty people.

Seated at the kitchen counter, reading a newspaper which was two days old, Michel greeted her with a wave of the Moka coffee pot and a smile.

"You slept well?" He poured her a coffee and refreshed his own.

"Very, very well," she said, joining him at the counter and accepting the welcome drink. "It's so peaceful here."

"That's partly why I put you downstairs. Four guys left at three this morning from upstairs, so that would not have been so peaceful. So, you will go into Chamonix today to make connections?"

"Yes, and Les Chosalets too."

Michel's chalet was actually in Argentière, a small town five miles up the valley from Chamonix and some 250 m higher. On its southern boundary, the campsite at Les Chosalets was the Camping du Glacier d'Argentière. Run by the Ravanel family, this was the camping location favoured by Jenny and her friends, so Argentière was a very familiar haunt. It was possible—and quite common—to turn up in this area solo and find other like-minded people to link up with for expeditions into the mountains. (It did require an element of care to ensure both compatibility and competence.)

"I can drop you in town—I have to go in this morning—and we can go by the camping."

"Oh, that would be great, thanks."

"Yes, I have to leave this afternoon to go to Arolla, *en Suisse*, for three days, Friday, Saturday, Sunday, but what will you do on

Monday and Tuesday? We could go to Le Dent du Géant then, if you wish."

"Oh, yes, please, if you're OK to do that."

This elegant mountain on the French-Italian border had been mentioned in the car last night on the way from the airport. At 4,013 m, it would represent a new landmark for Jenny.

"Yes, I have a break. And you hope to get up high at least twice before then, climbing in the Aiguilles maybe? And you will have been here for nearly a week. You will be acclimatised. Let's get you to beyond four thousand metres!"

She gave him a quick peck on the cheek and squeezed his arm and they both looked suitably pleased with the plan.

The Aiguilles, or "needles", of Chamonix were the most striking feature in the valley. A line of steep and jagged peaks of orange granite, they looked impossibly high and difficult and it was almost impossibly difficult to keep your eyes off them.

"It will be nice in Switzerland this evening, for it is Swiss National Day, the first of August. There will be a candlelit procession, a big fire, fireworks."

But for now, it was some bread and more coffee.

An hour later, Michel turned off the road at Les Chosalets towards the campsite. As they nosed slowly up the narrow lane, Jenny was delighted to be reminded of the familiar sights—the little chapel on the left, the water butt on the right—and then the campsite. She hopped out and went to the noticeboard next to the office, scanning it for any interesting messages and ready to add her own, which she had prepared before leaving.

The proprietor, M. Bernard Ravanel, approached the office with a large German shepherd on a short lead and gave her a hearty greeting.

"Bonjour! Ça va?"

Paper Chase

"Bonjour. Très bien, merci," she replied, pleased that he seemed to have recognised her.

"Cherchez de la place, encore une fois?"

"Non, merci, ma peut-être plus tard. J'habite chez Louison maintenant." She gestured to the car.

Bernard waved in recognition and then went over to chat to Michel as she finished up with the noticeboard.

Next, they headed into Chamonix and to the *Office*. Just above the main square and the bus station was a building which was the true centre of Chamonix, for many who were interested in the mountains: the *Maison de la Montagne*. A substantial, three-storey stone structure, it remained, with its windows thrown wide open, remarkably cool throughout the heat of the summer. The ground floor was the home of the office of the guides—the *Bureau des Guides*—where Michel was now heading. The first floor housed the *Météo*, providers of excellent weather information on at least a daily basis. Weather reports were regularly posted on the noticeboard opposite, but you could always pop in to raise a specific query. The top floor was the *Office de Haute Montagne*, a wonderful facility in which to research, plan, meet, or just pass part of a rest day in the cool. A large table with a bench either side was the central feature, and there were more than ample supplies of maps and guidebooks to bring over and peruse there. By its nature, it was a place to bump into old acquaintances or to make new friends and messages could be left for known or unknown parties in the *cahier des messages*. A member of staff was in evidence behind the desk to help with any queries and the most outstanding feature, quite literally, was the large relief model of the whole Mont Blanc massif. This was over to one side in a glass case at about waist level, so you could walk around it and see the topography you were planning to explore. A final benefit of this place was the toilet on the first floor—a "proper" toilet where you could sit down, rather than squat with your feet on the big ceramic footprints.

They said their farewells and agreed to meet on Sunday evening to finalise plans for the Dent du Géant trip. It was now Thursday. Michel entered the *Bureau des Guides*, and Jenny slung her small rucksack over her shoulder and headed upstairs.

Perhaps it had been a bit ambitious to think that serious planning could be done during such a short flight. In any event, Jenny was now refreshed and able to get down to business.

At one of Chamonix's many cafes, La Terrasse with its odd lilac colour and its much older, pillared structure, she had picked a spot next to the river. Her coffee was in the sun, but her notepad was in the shade of her own head and shoulders. The pleasant warmth of the sunshine was tempered by the cool air rushing to keep up with the River Arve. The Arve was broad in Chamonix yet still flowed so quickly that it could mesmerise, giving a dizzy feeling to anyone looking down from a bridge and watching the swift flow, even those accustomed to heights and danger. As well as the cool air of the glaciers, it carries abundant sediment, because of its speed, giving it its opaque shade of grey-green.

Sitting beneath the awesome picture postcard of the Chamonix Aiguilles, the "needles" of Chamonix, Jennifer Andrews prepared to consider how matters stood. Around her was all the bustle of a busy holiday resort, with the emphasis now very much on mountaineering, rather than skiing. It was bustling but not packed to the gunwales, as it could be at times in either summer or winter. Amid this bustle, it was the character of the trade which took precedence—not trade in a brash sense, like some garish market, but all-pervasive nevertheless. Every narrow number on the street was a shop or a cafe. The shops specialised in a way which was regarded as little more than nostalgic impracticality in the UK and the cafes spilled their ambience with their furniture on to the cobbles outside. It was a place of character, very human, very French.

Paper Chase

Back a step in the scale of things, to look at the town from outside its bustle of activity was to see more of Switzerland, as many would say. In fact, though, the architecture was that of the Alps, rather than any mere country, the product and reflection of the mountains themselves. Like the mountains, the buildings were rugged, because they had to be to survive. The post card images were seen through—this was not picturesque but stark practicality. From small cabins to large hotels, the emphasis was on the roof. These were not structures with roofs on top to keep out the weather, these were roofs with dwarf walls tucked somewhere underneath to connect them to the ground. These were buildings to withstand storm and deluge and to bear, at need, excessive weights of snow.

A ringing bell drew Jenny's eye to the other main type of building design—the church, with lofty spire stretching to pierce the sky even as the peaks of the mountains themselves do. From unusually flat shoulders, like the low pastures surrounding the mountains, the spire swept up like an exponential curve, aspiring to and inspired by the most daunting of the granite *aiguilles* above. Daunting they were to normal mortals yet irresistibly attractive to the eye—magnetic, awesome. From the elegant spire of le Petit Dru to the jagged Aiguille de Blaitière, from the Aiguille des Grands Charmoz above to the curiously inhabited Aiguille du Midi (accessible via its amazing cable car, or téléphérique), these marvellous pinnacles dominated the scene, towering so near, it seemed. Yet, with an eye to perspective, it could be seen that they themselves were dwarfed by the great mountains behind them—above all, Mont Blanc, the White Mountain.

Sipping the wonderful French coffee *(do they really know how to make coffee anywhere other than France and Italy?)*, Jenny forced herself to stop admiring her surroundings and consider the matter at hand.

She had discovered that Cameron Field was placing business through his general account which ought to have been transacted through the life division. Apparently, he had not created this situation, but he had been very slow to do anything about remedying it—if indeed he really had now. This was more important, in a way, as an indicator of the wrong sort of attitude, particularly bearing in mind what she had become aware of next. The next thing was that some of the business coming in through this channel and being wrongly categorised and managed within Morgan Field Associates was clearly fraudulent. Passport numbers ought to be unique. And personal identification numbers also ought to be unique. That was the third thing: Cameron Field now had two of these, the second one having been set up very shortly after an honest member of staff had raised concerns about the possibility of a loophole in the new system. From what Jenny had seen, it was not necessarily the only loophole. She had discovered information at branch level which ought to have been available only at a higher level. Perhaps it had not been very fulsome information, but she could not help thinking that she should not have been able to find out anything from the lower level about the upper.

However, the headline news from the Mike Thomas file was that Cameron Field was in partnership with Jerram in the J-Cash Services business. He was downplayed as a sort of sleeping partner, but even so. This was not Morgan Field but C. W. Field, Esq. It had come out in a declaration of interest, which he had been required to make, but since it did not concern a Morgan Field client it had apparently not raised any eyebrows—apart from hers. And if it was not a Morgan Field client, why had a client account been set up? Was it another example of careless or expedient accounting practice or something more sinister?

She stretched and rose to signal to the waitress for another coffee. The shade within the cafe was so pronounced that cigarettes glowed in the gloom.

Paper Chase

No one was near enough to glance at the notepad on the terrace table and no one cared anyway. The top sheet, flickering slightly in the breeze, showed:

IGBIN	JERRAM	FIELD	OTHER??
Fraudulent "dread disease" policies	J-Cash (Dad!)	Partnership with Jerram??	CWF/MRD liaison? Bluffing?!
Some already converted - where did the proceeds go? - how?	CWF file … IN PARTNERSHIP— J & CWF, <u>Esq</u>	Breaking the rules - Igbin -LIFE business - J-Cash through MFA??	Morgan Family—move to flotation?!
Kept in "wrong place" by CWF - how much did he know?	Mystery building - Balerno Hill T E - Doesn't exist? - Cyprus/CWF?!	2nd PIN created! - authorised BHTE - payments to CYPRUS? - how much??	Negative feedback re: "new" computer system …
		All the rumours of him having too much money? No smoke without fire?? Do I know him at all?	

The cool of the river had become rather less welcome by the time Jenny straightened again, rubbing stiff shoulders and folding up her papers. Was she any further forward?

The file from Mike Thomas had contained three slim bundles of papers and also a CD, as she had felt in the envelope. What more could the CD tell her? Where could she read it? Would there be a computer in the library? And then she remembered that she had seen a sign for something new: Chamonix's first "Internet Cafe". The idea was that you could rent a computer for a short time. The real idea was that it was a computer which was dialled in to the internet, of course. She had not paid it any attention at the time, but now it seemed a great idea and she could remember just about where it was that she had seen the place. She could afford to use a few francs for this, whether or not she needed the internet, so that was where she headed.

There was a lot on the disk, but most was not directly relevant to what was troubling her at present. After expending 30 francs, however, she had been able to have a quick look through and to resolve one specific query. Cameron Field—actually, Cameron Field no. 2—had authorised payments of £10,000 per month for the lease of a building. She could not find any trace of the building, but the payments were being made to a numbered account in Cyprus associated with J-Cash Services, a business in which he was apparently a partner, under a client account which ought not to have existed. *(Wow!)*

She wondered what might happen while she was away—in other words, what might have happened by the time she returned. It did not appear that any of this was truly time critical, however. No one else was aware that she had this knowledge and there seemed no need for her to try to raise the alarm remotely from here. There would be time enough when she was back on the 19th, she thought.

She would have to speak to Mike about it then, though, and presumably would have to go over the head of her senior sponsor for the audit to his main board.

What am I doing trying to work this out in France? she thought. She wouldn't have been able to begin to explain this to anyone else. She couldn't even explain it to herself.

However, it was now Thursday and she would be officially on leave after tomorrow.

And tomorrow, she would go climbing, leaving all of this behind.

CHAPTER

23

MOUNTAINEERING COUNCIL OF SCOTLAND

Thursday, 1 August 1996, 08:00

Mark and Simon were pleased not to be setting off on the long, steep tramp up the Cobbler again this morning. Three days in a row would have been too much. They had been back up the mountain the day before, in better weather, and had ticked off Ardgartan Arête as planned, adding to their schedule a rather harder route on the South Peak, Ithuriel's Wall, to justify their effort in getting up there again. Today would be a lazy day.

"What are you scribbling away at?" Mark wanted to know. "Are you keeping a journal now?"

"No!"

For a moment or two, it seemed as if that was to be the entirety of Simon's answer, but then he continued.

"I was getting a bit of background on this woman for Jenny. It seems she's an independent sales agent for the place Jenny's working at the moment—Morgan Field Associates—but she's also a partner in a law firm, which is a bit of an odd combo, isn't it?"

"I don't know. Is it?" Watermark did not seem too interested.

"Well, it is, yes. And for Morgan Field, there's something about only liaising with the boss man, Cameron Field. If I could get in to meet him, I might be able to find out a bit more for her just by snooping around or asking him an odd question, see how he reacts—or just by good luck. What's-it-dippity."

They had just finished breakfast and the stove was cool enough now to pack away, which is what Simon had begun to do as he was talking. Mark sat on the tailgate and thumbed through a guidebook.

"I got the impression Jenny was in a bit of a hurry, but I think she said she was down in London today. Don't know when she's back in Edinburgh."

"Not any time soon," Mark put in. "She's in Chamonix."

"What? Oh, yes, 'April Fool'! Oh, no—first of August, it is."

"No, seriously. Look." Always happy to have an excuse to show off his mobile phone, Mark fished it out and switched it on. "I've just had an SMS message from her—see?"

Simon peered at the small screen in the upper part of the phone and made out the letters:

> GONE CHAM EARLY.
> THERE NOW. SEE
> YOU LATER. J.

"Oh, sod it! Let's go and join her, then," was Simon's conclusion. "I was going to suggest it anyway, but I didn't think she was off for a while yet."

"Hey, we could, couldn't we? That would be great!" Mark was suddenly enthusiastic. "Drive down?"

"Yeah. I've got a ferry ticket. I can use it any time, even peak times. Just need to book twenty-four hours in advance. I won it in a competition."

"What are you like?"

"Car and two passengers. Stena—Southampton to Cherbourg. No problem!"

"Hey, what about this Cameron Field, though?"

"Sod him!"

Paper Chase

"Why don't we go and see him on the way? It's only an hour and a half or something from here. Jenny's not going to be there. No one knows us. We can say it's about some new business or something to get in. Those guys are always after new business, aren't they?"

In fact, they had gone for a stroll around the shore of the loch for a while and had had an early lunch before they had set off.

"That was great climbing on the Cobbler," Wacko said.

"Preferred Dumbarton Rock. No knackering walk-in. Or Swanage," Watermark replied.

"You're soft. Soft southerners…"

The day after the curry, they had gone climbing on the sea cliffs at Swanage, staying there overnight and having a full day's climbing there the next day, Saturday. Then they'd had a day of driving to get as far as Glasgow and spent the next day on the wonderful Dumbarton Rock with no walk-in. Mark was beginning to have difficulty remembering what day it was. That meant Tuesday and Wednesday on the Cobbler, and today was indeed Thursday. It was not April Fool's Day, as Simon had first said, but it was the first of A—the first of August.

Wacko: full of contradictions. He could appear less than competent or could seem to make life difficult for himself when it didn't really matter. When it did matter, he just got better.

Mark recalled one example from several years ago, one of the first times he, Wacko, and Jenny had gone climbing together, in North Wales. They'd been in Jenny's car.

From Mark's point of view as driver, it went like this: They were on a long, straight section of road with good visibility. The road was broad and clear and the weather fine. In the distance, a deer darted out from the left and crossed the road. An approaching car failed to avoid the deer and then stopped.

The blue Nissan in front of Mark hesitated but then realised that there was clearly enough space to pass and no point in stopping. With a good section of the straight still remaining, Mark was already closing slightly with the intention of overtaking once past the obstruction. At this point, the Nissan braked suddenly and came to a stop almost opposite the other car. It had scarcely stopped, however, when it was propelled forward again.

Even with the ABS fitted to Jenny's car, there was no way Mark could stop in time when he had already been accelerating to some extent.

To Mark, it was as though it all happened in slow motion. He had made his judgment previously about how things would play out—the car would pass the obstruction; he would pass the car—but now had to revise that thinking and seemed to have plenty of time to do so. On his left, there was a broad verge of patchy grass with a forty-five-degree kerbstone and then a ramp of earth, which sloped down gently to the edge of the field, perhaps a metre lower. Between these, there was no wire fence but a light and intermittent low hedge. He assessed the possibility of swerving on to the verge to avoid the stopping car. The "magic solution" would be to swerve past the Nissan on the verge, which was just about wide enough, and then rejoin the carriageway with a sigh of relief (or equivalent). He felt, however, that he would catch the earth bank and end up in the field. Moreover, he felt that—at the speed they were going—the transfer to the softer and less even surface would be too much and he would actually end upside down in the field, having rolled several times, probably with one or more broken necks in the car. His considered decision was to have a "safe" accident, and he applied himself to reducing his speed as much as he possibly could and keeping the car in a straight line.

How many milliseconds this all took, he did not know, but—obviously, in this melee round—he had no time to share these thoughts with his fellow travellers. They became aware of the situation on impact, though, if not before.

Mark was aware that he could see things which had not been there before. There was the car in front, of course, the blue Nissan, now very much closer and at a slight angle, but there were other things as well: a magazine promoting a shining BMW;

a credit card jammed so hard between the rubber and the fascia at the bottom of the windscreen that it later proved difficult to remove; a large, white airbag, despite which his shoulder hurt from the restraining effect of his seat belt.

Simon broke the silence. "That was a bad one!" he said. "Are you OK, Jen?"

As he turned, Mark could see he had a gash on his forehead—no airbag on his side.

"Yes, I'm fine," she mumbled.

"Mark?"

"Yes, I'm OK, thanks."

"OK, just take it easy and make sure you're all right as you start to move around."

Simon opened the door and eased himself out on to the verge and then to the Nissan in front. The two ladies in it—a mother and daughter, apparently—were shocked, shaken, but seemingly uninjured. Simon returned to the union of the two vehicles and then walked around the Nissan to the offside, assessing the damage. By this time, his two companions had got out of the car and Mark joined him by the front wheel.

"It doesn't look too bad," Simon opined. This comment was intended to represent their car, as the rear of the wheel arch of the Nissan seemed to be very firmly in contact with the rear offside tyre. There was no sign of other traffic and the car on the opposite side of the road, bizarrely, had disappeared.

Simon went to the verge to check on Jenny and Mark got back in the car and tried to start it, but to no avail—it was dead. He couldn't seem to be able to think what else to do, so he just sat still.

"Try it again," Simon instructed.

Mark was aware that Simon had been doing something. He followed the instruction and, this time, the engine started.

"Immobiliser," Simon offered in attempted explanation.

Mark gently reversed and—despite worrying initial sound effects—the cars separated. The hazard lights were on, but Mark didn't remember switching them on.

Two cars had passed by then—one each way—but had not stopped. After a brief further inspection, and after having exchanged details with the car in front, they limped to the next town, Simon now driving. There, they located a local mechanic's business to get an initial assessment of the damage, and—as promised—called the AA for the two women.

Wacko had quietly stepped up to the plate. He had taken charge of the situation and had made all the right decisions. And this was despite—as it turned out—having had quite a bad concussion at the time. Wacko: often misunderstood, Mark thought, but definitely a handy man to have around in a tight spot.

On paper, Jean Stovell would not have been one of the most senior employees at Morgan Field Associates. However, having worked for the firm for longer than anyone else and, what's more, being the personal assistant to the managing director, she actually had extraordinary influence.

Given that the MD was based in the Edinburgh office, it had not seemed necessary to have an actual branch manager in post as well, as in their other locations. Instead, they had John Wade, whose role—in addition to his normal broking duties—was to handle most of the routine administration, including low-level recruitment, performance appraisals and the like. Of course, they had not put it to him in these terms and had sought rather to aggrandise his title of "office manager". He approached Jean now, a bulky folder under his arm.

"Is it OK if I use Cameron's office for a little while? When do you expect him back? I just have a couple of private calls to make."

The rest of the office was open plan. She knew he was involved in a recruitment exercise at present and may have such a need.

Paper Chase

She also knew the little prick probably just wanted to sit in the big chair and try to look important for a while. However, Cameron wasn't expected back in the office today.

"I don't think Mr Field will be back before five," she said, and of course this was true.

He stepped into the office, closing the door behind him, and made himself at home. Twenty minutes later, she had to tap at the door (against her better judgment) and ask if he would see two gentlemen about a prospective piece of new business, the Mountaineering Council of Scotland, as no one from the development team was in the office at present. *Yes, he'll see them. Big man, him!* she thought and went to bring the two gentlemen through.

"Right, hang on ... make yourselves comfortable. I've got a questionnaire which will help at my ... in my development team's area. Two ticks."

He scuttled off and Watermark took a step towards the smoked-glass wall, half screening Wacko as he did so. The secretary was facing outwards and no one else was paying any attention. How much could they see anyway? Behind him, he heard the filing cabinet open quickly, almost before he had registered these details.

Wacko had seen his chance and had taken it, casually opening the second drawer of the four-drawer cabinet as naturally as glancing out of the window (had there been one). As he had expected, (1) the files were clearly labelled, and (2) this drawer contained roughly the second quarter of the alphabet, including— fortunately—the file he was looking for. Locating the Igbin file easily, he simply took its contents, contained in a neat, cardboard folder, leaving the suspended file and its coloured label intact. Sliding the drawer shut, he added this cardboard folder to the smaller bundle of papers he already had and, without a word, the pair sat down at the table in the corner. He had noticed that the file behind the one he had taken had been entitled "JERRAM".

"Cheers!" Mark had arrived back at the table with two pints of 80/- and Simon greeted him appropriately before taking a deep swig. He kept the bundle of papers beside him on the bench seat, undisturbed and unread. They deserved a quick drink.

"What are you like!" Mark's voice was jocular but low. "You suddenly decide out of the blue that we represent a national body for climbing?"

"You could see the way it was going. They thought it was just us and they don't deign to get involved in 'personal business'."

"But you said we were MCS and then flashed your AAC membership card as authority. Hmm … Mountaineering Council of Scotland and Austrian Alpine Club—so easy to get those two mixed up."

"It's just like having a clipboard—look as though you mean it and they'll never check."

"Yes, but then you only grab the whole file of papers. That's really subtle."

"OK, they'll notice eventually, but then it's 'Who had that file out last?' and 'Why?' and whatever. Stuff gets lost and misfiled in offices all the time."

"I suppose …"

"Anyway, I was glad you remembered our 'urgent appointment', when it was starting to get as boring as a biscuit."

"You mean when his little form started asking for more information than we could plausibly make up?"

"Yeah, that too. Although, I think he was a bit out of his depth as well. He seemed so pleased to dish out his little cards and let us go."

"Yes." Mark looked at his copy. "'Office Manager John Wade ACII'," he read out. "I hope he doesn't expect too much new business from that meeting."

"Hey, talking of which, can you imagine working in a place like that every day? And that guy downstairs—what kind of a job is that?"

Paper Chase

"Can you imagine his job description? Job title: security guard? Caretaker?"

"Reports to: head of security," Simon put in.

Mark continued, getting into the swing of it, "Place of work: variable, but mainly downstairs lobby. Principal duties: wear basic uniform, stand around and say good morning to people."

"Must be prepared occasionally to press the lift's call button (rather ostentatiously) and then retreat," Wacko added.

"Other duties as required to achieve corporate objectives. Personal attributes: must be bright (although not in an intellectual way) and *mainly* inoffensive."

"I could do *that* job," Simon laughed, "but maybe not *every* day. Hey, and it reminds me of something I heard on the radio as I was coming to pick you up to go to Swanage. Did you hear it? It was extracts from a book all about quirky old Britain by this guy called Bill Bryson."

Watermark shook his head and gave a "no idea" shrug with his hands, so Simon went on.

"This chap is a journalist from the States, but he's lived here for years. He was making fun of British oddities from an American's point of view. The bit I liked, though, was when he was saying how stupid pigeons were. He was in a railway station and he got on to a bit of a rant about it and it was as funny as a rabbit."

Mark raised an eyebrow but tried not to interrupt.

"He summarised it by saying, 'Right—here are the instructions for being a pigeon: One, peck at something inappropriate, such as a cigarette end. Two, suddenly take fright and fly off on to a high girder. Three, shit. Four, repeat.' It was really funny. I must see if they've got the book in the library—*Notes from a Small Island*, I think it was."

As they left thoughts of unlikely job descriptions and instructions for life behind, Simon glanced around the typical, old-fashioned Edinburgh pub: high ceilings, ornate hardwood, tiles, mirrors, moderately busy. At a table quite nearby in the corner sat a huge man dressed in black, tall but also very heavy.

His companion was young and fidgety and seemed to be awaiting instructions. The big man regarded a small piece of paper, which he had unfolded, for what seemed too long a time before looking up at his companion, also for a long moment, and then Simon heard a rather menacing voice.

"Aye, ye always were a propitious wee bastert."

"What's 'propitious' mean, then?"

"Away and ask somebody that cares!" offered the big man whilst transferring his bulk from the table to the bar, to be understood more as "Dismissed!" than as an offer to buy anyone drinks.

Jerram was not inclined to magnanimity.

Even the laid-back Simon Jackson found this man somehow disconcerting. He certainly did not want to attract his attention. If he had known as much about him as Jennifer Andrews did, he would have been even more concerned.

CHAPTER
24

JERRAM

Thursday, 1 August 1996, 14:15

Cameron Field's office had been empty, allowing John Wade to entertain his new business prospects, as Field had left early afternoon, telling Jean Stovell he would not be back that day. He had not felt it necessary to tell her that he had a 2 p.m. meeting with his solicitor.

"OK," Cameron said. "Jerram's organisation has been the subject of enquiries by the police, from time to time, but I'm satisfied that it's now a decent organisation. One, while there have been enquiries, I'm not aware of any prosecutions and two, it's the kind of business where you can be exposed to a rogue member of staff taking shortcuts, going too far, breaking the rules, whatever you want to call it. It's not unique in that regard either, let me tell you. The same is true, in reality, for any organisation where you are trying to manage people—to achieve objectives through others. Anyway, the thing is that the service they provide is one that's needed and is becoming increasingly so. There are lots of people who just live from month to month or week to week, never have any savings or money to spare and don't have the right kind of background or abilities to jump through the hoops held up by the banks. So, when a bit of unexpected expense comes along, it has a disproportionately damaging effect on them. If you or I suddenly needed new shock absorbers or something, we'd get them, pay with a credit card and settle the credit card bill at our leisure. I'm sure, like me, you would just pay the bill when it came in, but you would have the option to park it there for a month or two, if you wanted to.

"The bottom line is, you'd just get the work done, because you're good for it. The people I'm talking about don't even have credit cards. They either don't qualify for one or they've had one withdrawn from them in the past. They're regarded as '*not* good for it'. What they can get through J-Cash Services is just a small, unsecured loan to tide them over. In ninety per cent of the cases, it's paid back within weeks, if not days, whenever the next pay comes along, and then the people scrimp and save again and make do from there. Yes, the APR is a bit higher than, say, a bank loan over three years or something, but one, it's a different kind of arrangement; two, it's over a much shorter period, so the actual amount of interest is not normally high; and three, these are generally people who couldn't get a loan from a bank, even if it would be the solution to their problem, which it's not."

He paused for breath, realising that he was not just justifying his business connection with someone whom he regarded, privately, as rather unsavoury. He believed what he was saying and knew that there was a segment of society for which this ability to use J-Cash Services to push and pull the finances a little was very important. This is why he had been pontificating about it in a public lecture all those months ago, he supposed, and why Jerram had spoken to him, had picked him out.

How had he originally come to work with Jerram? It had started just over a year ago, when Dave Sieger had walked into his office one day and asked if he had a minute …

When Sieger finished explaining, Cameron Field paused, undecided, for a few moments. Dave Sieger was his youngest and least experienced account executive, but then again, he had achieved that lofty status at only 25 on merit and because he was clever and talented and conscientious. So, couldn't he sort this matter out for himself? However, Cameron knew the client, Francis Vaughan, to be a tricky, slippery customer and Morgan Field couldn't afford to end up with (allegedly) £14,000 worth of good quality carpet if it all went pear shaped.

He still couldn't quite believe it. Sieger had been trying to collect an outstanding debt of just over £14,000 and Vaughan, apparently in all seriousness, had offered him a roll of Afghan carpet instead. Although he had not said so, it had occurred to Cameron that he would not be surprised if there was a dead body inside that roll of carpet, as in *The Godfather.* Thankfully, Sieger had declined, but had been unable to agree an outcome which involved the immediate transfer of actual sterling to clear the overdue account.

"All right, I know Francis Vaughan is an awkward little toerag." Cameron made his decision. "Fix another appointment to see him and let him know I'll be coming with you. See Jean about dates. We'll read him the Riot Act and come up with a way forward, one way or the other."

Vaughan ran an array of interlinked companies under BV Holdings and was actually quite a significant earner for them—when he paid his debts. Everything always seemed to be on a bit of a knife's edge with Vaughan, however. Relieved, Dave Sieger went off to get some dates from Jean first of all and then try to make the arrangement to visit again.

Jean reminded Cameron a few days later that he was due to be making the visit but then annoyed him by pointing out that Dave Sieger was off sick, having sustained whiplash injuries in a car accident the previous evening. After initially telling her to cancel the appointment, Cameron countermanded the instruction. He would go. He wanted this concluded.

This was not the most salubrious of Edinburgh locations, even for Granton, and Cameron Field did his best to avoid puddles and determined-looking weeds as he walked through the car park. He had parked about as close as he could and now walked past unhitched trailers alongside what appeared to be an abandoned warehouse. At its southern end were some inauspicious offices, which nevertheless did show signs of life. A door bearing the faded letters "BV" was propped open by a fire extinguisher and the small lobby it opened on to comprised a locked inner door and a shuttered counter. He rang for attention.

Having arrived five minutes early for the arranged appointment, he was not at all pleased to be told that Mr Vaughan was out of town and was not expected back that day. As there was little more to be said, the shutters closed again and he was left a little stunned. It then got dark.

Turning to the door, he saw that the frame was filled by a man dressed in black who appeared to be larger than it in all directions. After a moment, the man stepped back to allow him to exit.

As he did so, the man said, "Probably my fault, I'm afraid, if there was a sudden change of plans."

He had clearly heard the exchange with the BV "receptionist".

"I was quite keen to catch up with Frankie-boy myself, but I suspect he wasn't so keen. Or maybe it was just that he owed you a lot of money."

Normally, Cameron Field would have engaged as little as possible in this kind of situation, but he was both irritated and slightly intrigued and so he said, "You couldn't actually make it up! He owes me fourteen thousand pounds and he offered a member of my staff a roll of carpet."

"Ah, that's our Frankie-boy. But never mind. I'll take care of it for you. He leases this building (and one or two others) from me, so I'll add it to his charges."

"But will the lease allow for that?" Cameron was surprised to hear himself retort.

Paper Chase

"Oh, it doesn't matter quite so much what it actually says in the lease as whether Mr Vaughan believes I'm happy or not. I'm already slightly unhappy, as I've come to see him—like you—and he's not here. You'll have your fourteen thousand in a few days. Frankie-boy can give me the payment details and tell me the exact sum and then he'll pay it back to me along with his other charges—and a little interest—within the next three months." Before Cameron could think of an appropriate response, the man went on. "But perhaps you can do me a favour in return? You see, I know your line of business, Mr Field, and also your inclination towards social responsibility."

Was it something about his size, his slow-paced but rather menacing voice, or some other factor? You just were not going to brush him aside and say, "Well, must dash, things to do," and he knew it. Was he just seeing how far he could go?

"You see, I've been a big fan of Johnny Cash for almost as long as I can remember. I went to see him in Nashville, just a few months ago in the autumn. I must say, he was excellent. But that's not what I wanted to talk to you about. He's exactly thirteen years older than I am, you know, Johnny Cash. Anyway, while I was there, I met a fellow businessman from further east in Tennessee—man called Jones. Turned out we had a lot in common. He has set up a new business called 'Check into Cash'. Funny, that, because I went to Nashville to 'check into Cash'—Johnny Cash." He smiled. "But, you see, it's an American 'check'—a cheque"—he gestured with his enormous hands—"and the business is booming. The cheque thing is just that they write a cheque and the business agrees not to cash it yet. You see, it's about the provision of short-term, unsecured loans, effectively—just the kind of thing needed by those poor folk you were talking about in your lecture at the chamber of commerce recently—the ones that the banks don't favour."

This man attended chamber meetings? If so, surely Cameron would have seen him. He was a hard man to miss, in more ways than one.

"But you know all this," the man continued, "because you mentioned Jones and his company in your talk. What I was thinking was that it might be possible to underwrite the risk of the odd loan going bad. I've been involved in loans in the past—either on purpose or ... incidentally—but I'm planning to launch it as a different kind of venture, you see, as in the States. I'd still be taking care and having the expectation that loans would be repaid all right, but I could follow a more liberal strategy if I knew that there was some form of indemnity in place—for example, if someone just disappeared—rather than having to ... enforce the arrangement through my own organisation. So much of that kind of business is about perceptions, you see. We could have a broader reach and run at lower cost if some of the risk aspects could be taken out of it, so that would potentially bring a double benefit to those needy souls who can't make ends meet in the short term and just need temporary support from time to time. I was proposing to call this J-Cash Services, by the way. You see, it sort of fits to its genesis." He smiled again. "And I know you think the service is necessary ..."

Cameron did think something of the kind was necessary—he wouldn't have been lecturing at the chamber of commerce about it otherwise—but he was now thinking of underwriting this himself, rather than through a formal insurance route, in which he could see many difficulties. He had the resources and would be happy to see some of them being put to a good cause. He really wanted to find a way to put them to good use.

"I think I may be able to come up with a way to meet what I think you're looking for," he began, "but it would be only within certain parameters. We would have to have an understanding, for the underwriters, of amounts and how and to whom and on what terms they would be offered and so on. But I think I may be able to do something for you. Leave it with me to do a little research."

"Now, that sounds quite encouraging." Even these words and his most avuncular tone seemed somehow threatening. "You'll let me know? As soon as you have anything?"

Paper Chase

"And you are ...?"

"Jerram," he pronounced, handing over a card.

The interview was over, it seemed, for he turned and departed—apparently unhurriedly but surprisingly quickly—disappearing around the other side of the building to the west.

Cameron looked at the card in his hand. It was the size and thickness of a business card but was completely blank apart from a telephone number written in blue ink.

Based on that discussion, they came to an arrangement within a few weeks. Cameron gained a much clearer understanding about the J-Cash business model and the stated modus operandi and the agreement was essentially that, if business was conducted within these parameters, a substantial proportion (it varied slightly, but around 85 per cent) of any bad debts would be met by the underwriters. To facilitate this, an advance was provided, from which loans were made—a little like a loan from the underwriters to J-Cash. Reports would be fed back monthly and the amount of this "float" would be topped up, like a sort of escrow account. Effectively, Jerram ran J-Cash and Field bankrolled him.

Very little was actually recorded in writing and certainly nothing in the form of a binding contract. The way Jerram had explained his relationship with Francis Vaughan seemed to inform this. As a by-product of the arrangement, Morgan Field never again had any difficulty in collecting amounts due from the BV Holdings companies. Field was aware that Sieger now regarded him as some kind of magician, in terms of credit control, and had not kept that opinion entirely to himself.

The J-Cash arrangement moved on apace, with regular monthly reports and cash amounts toing and froing. If Jerram had any idea that it was C. W. Field, Esq. supporting his business—not some professional insurance syndicate, which would have required much more formal paperwork, surely—he said nothing and maintained the pretence.

"Anyway," Field explained to his solicitor, "there's probably not much more to be done just now. I don't mind too much helping the boys in blue with their enquiries, but I wanted you on board in case it gets any more serious. However, I am quite confident that they have no need to be troubling me again and would be wasting their time—as well as mine—if they did."

He had mentioned that his only misdeed had been transacting the J-Cash escrow account through his company's records but that it did not really cost anything to do so. The company could perhaps stand him that little perk, in any case. Of more concern had been the fact that it amounted to misleading Jerram into thinking that he had the benefit of an insurance contract, whereby he could have the expectation that substantial, guaranteed funds would be there to support the agreement entered into. This was not ideal, but as the solicitor already knew for other reasons, there was little likelihood of C. W. Field being unable to meet his obligations under the agreement, either now or in the foreseeable future, bearing in mind the small amounts involved, regardless of the potential volume of them. He was a wealthy man.

"Well, that is good, of course," his solicitor replied. "I know you said the police were not disclosing very much to you, but it did sound, from the line of questioning you set out to me, as though there was perhaps some concern other than merely the business connection with J-Cash Services. Is there anyone you can think of who would have reason to pass libellous material to the police, perhaps simply to cause mischief?"

Field thought of the audit and then could not really imagine why. That was a potential irritant, perhaps, but it was just business, not a matter for the police. "No, I really can't. If that turns out to be the case, we could sue the … let's say miscreant, couldn't we?"

"Yes, certainly, but it would perhaps warrant a little thought in advance for four main reasons. Firstly, we may never find out who the 'informant' is, either because the police are disinclined to provide the information or because he is genuinely anonymous to them. Secondly, libel cases are really rather difficult to prosecute successfully. Thirdly, even a success could represent a pyrrhic victory, as potential settlements are capped at a low level and as there is also often an inclination on the part of the judiciary to make token awards. Finally and just as importantly, the publicity the process gives to the original allegations, even when proved to be unfounded or vexatious, can still be damaging."

"You make that prospect sound very attractive indeed." Sarcasm dripped from Field's assessment.

"Well, that is something for possible consideration in the future, in any event. Hopefully, this whole consultation may prove to be purely precautionary, but do let me know if you are contacted by the police again. I shall, of course, be happy to attend and represent you directly and I would strongly recommend that course of action in any future dialogue which you may have with them."

"I hear you. I could have called you yesterday, but I really thought it was better just to speak to them and—if they have any sense—let them know they're barking up the wrong tree."

Although it was still only the middle of the afternoon, he had indicated to Jean Stovell that he would not be back in the office that day and he had no intention of changing his mind. A few hours of good, productive work this morning had allowed him to catch up with his short-term priorities, following the interruption of the previous afternoon. Now, he had a few personal matters to attend to.

CHAPTER
25

LA TRAVERSÉE DU GRÉPON

vendredi, 2 août 1996, 07:50

The trip to the *Office* yesterday had been productive. Jenny had been reviewing a note from a girl named Francesca in the *cahier des messages*, trying to get as much information as she could from the two versions there—the original Italian, which she could mostly understand, and the English version, which was shorter and simpler but not exactly right. It sounded a promising lead, though. Just then, she was interrupted by the girl who had left the note—or rather, by her climbing partner.

"Ah, you're reading our note," said a tall, strong-looking, self-assured woman with light-brown hair. She was obviously Scandinavian, and she introduced herself as Liv, from Denmark. "And this is Fran." She presented her smaller, slimmer, darker, quieter companion and they sat down and chatted together.

After a while, they all wrote down their names and where they were staying before they forgot to do so. Olivia Hansen and Francesca Borgesio were based at the Camping du Glacier d'Argentière—at Les Chosalets! They had been doing some climbing together, having met up only a week or so ago, but now Liv was meeting her regular partner from Sweden, leaving Fran at a loose end. Jenny and Fran had got on well and had appeared

Paper Chase

to be of a similar standard and so the plan had been hatched for today's outing.

Now, with her heart thumping and her body craving oxygen and rest, Jenny wondered if it had been a good idea. She knew it was, really, but Fran had been here for a week already and was bound to be going a bit better than Jenny was.

Liv, who had a car, had kindly run them into Chamonix for an early téléphérique up towards the Aiguille du Midi but only as far as the halfway station, the Plan de l'Aiguille. This was the large, uneven terrace along the feet of these rocky "needles", 1,500 m above Chamonix but 1,000 m below the peaks of the Aiguilles themselves. After traversing along from the cable car station, crossing several steep, lateral moraines of loose rock, she and Fran roped up for the ascent of the troubled Nantillons glacier. This small, steep glacier was very well endowed with dangerous crevasses, seemingly at all angles, and was certainly a place which required care. Still, they gained height rapidly, as Jenny's lungs could confirm.

For multiple people to move together on the glacier, the shortened length of rope between them has to remain taut—or at least, not slack—meaning that all members of the party are required to move at the same speed. Fran was leading at present and doing so very competently, Jenny thought, even though she was finding the pace a little difficult.

They could see their mountain clearly from here—the Aiguille du Grépon, higher but further back than its neighbours, its crenellated ramparts now looking enticing indeed.

Before long, just three hours after leaving the téléphérique station, they were at the foot of their objective, trying to see a way to cross the rimaye to move from the glacier to the smoothed rock beyond. This was achieved more easily than it had looked and they then began to scramble up the Charmoz-Grépon couloir, a steep gully of large stones and boulders. When heavily covered in binding snow, this was a straightforward ascent, stable and with footholds readily available wherever required. This late in the season, however, there was almost no snow to be seen and much more care was needed. Even the large boulders felt potentially loose and there was the feeling that the whole steep slope could avalanche without too much provocation. Jenny and Fran, therefore, tiptoed up as delicately as they could and tried to deny the slope that provocation.

Above this, on solid granite, the climbing was stupendous. The initial pitch was hard and in the shade, but then they gained the ridge and the sunshine. For pitch after pitch, they exchanged the lead, moving quickly on but thoroughly enjoying it. The line took them through an amazing variety of moves. Great flakes and solid blocks of perfect, rough, orange granite greeted them as they continued and they wove a line from the Nantillons (or Chamonix) side of the ridge to the Envers (or Mer de Glace) side and back again, through constant changes of view and perspective. Jenny was aware that snippets of Mahler's seventh symphony had been running through her head all day.

Finally reaching the true summit, at 3,482 m, with its small statue of the Madonna—quite common in France—they congratulated one another heartily. Jenny nearly burst into tears. She didn't know why; just felt so jubilant to be there.

After nearly making an error on the way down, they did remember the route they had read up on the day before and traversed along the ridge a bit further before making two abseils to easier ground. They carefully picked their way back down the Nantillons glacier, achieving almost the same route as on the way up, and then dispensed with the ropes and almost jogged along the lower path to the téléphérique station, arriving with about twenty-five minutes to spare for the last car back down.

It was worth the extra effort not to have the long walk down to the valley. Jenny sometimes agonised about this, but she was capable of performing the strenuous hillwalking. In a remote area, with no such extravagant mechanical aids, she would have to do so. However, here, where the mechanical access was in place, it seemed a pity not to make use of it when your freshness and

Paper Chase

fitness could be deployed on *wonderful* routes like the traverse of the Grépon, instead of on hours of climbing up or down a heavily wooded hillside.

This was *especially* so when one had only two weeks' leave to work with that year and the weather could either be kind—like today—or rather less so.

Half slumped over the rail in the busy cable car, their rucksacks between their feet, Fran and Jenny enjoyed the fresh air coming through the open window vents, but they were sufficiently fatigued to save any discussion—their exchanges of appreciation and reminiscences of a great day out—for when they were down in the valley and comfortably seated with cold beers in front of them. What a day! Jenny felt exhausted but somehow also much fitter than she had that morning.

Of course, they still had to get back to Argentière and their chauffeur of this morning was now off on an adventure of her own. So, they stopped at a single beer and left food for later, though they had been tempted by the trays of chips at a nearby table. They shouldered their packs once more and left the bustle of the centre for the main road up the valley.

They had covered less than a mile when a Swiss couple, heading over the pass to Martigny, stopped and picked them up. There was always a strong chance of a lift on this section of road, particularly when many of the motorists were fellow mountaineers.

Although it was only Jenny's first night, they dined out in Argentière at Luigi's—probably the best restaurant in the town—rather than observing the more normal practice of arranging some kind of camp or chalet meal. Tomorrow would be a rest day, but they agreed to meet up and review their options.

"Buona notte!"

"Arrivederci!"

CHAPTER

26

TRÉ-LE-CHAMP WEDDING

samedi, 3 août 1996, 10:30

It was very hot again, especially when moving steeply uphill, and Jenny and Fran took advantage of some shade whenever they could. Moving up the valley beyond Argentière, they had turned off the road on to a footpath on the left. This cut out several large hairpin bends on the road, provided them with some shade in the wooded areas and was generally quieter and more pleasant walking, although they did still have to cross the road more than once. They were headed for the village of Tré-le-Champ, where they would break away from the main valley and climb into the Aiguilles Rouges. Substantial mountains in their own right, the Aiguilles Rouges formed the north-west side of the valley and afforded excellent views of the main peaks on the opposite side, to the south-east.

Jenny had walked down to Les Chosalets quite early, when it was light but still chilly. She'd brought some bread and honey and Fran had already had the stove on for coffee with plenty of water in the pot, expecting company. So, they had had breakfast together, sitting on the grass outside Fran's tent, each glad to be wearing a warm fleece. The sun rose later in the mountains, because of the height of the horizon. Over their second cups of coffee, they had watched the sunshine travelling up the campsite towards

Paper Chase

their feet as the sun itself gradually rose over the shoulder of the Aiguille du Chardonnet behind them. By the time it had reached them, causing them to strip off the outer clothing immediately, their plans for the next few days had been in place.

Michel had said Jenny should stay as long as she wished and they had arranged to meet on his return on Sunday evening to prepare for the Dent du Géant trip. It had felt a bit awkward when he wasn't there, though, and she felt rather separated both from Fran and from the others within Michel's chalet. (They had not even discussed terms yet for her stay.)

Fran had a roomy "tunnel" tent, which she and Liv had been using but in which she was now alone. It was the kind of tent that would be no good at all on the mountain but was really comfortable on the campsite. It was a little more expensive for camp fees than *"une petite tente"* but probably worth it. She had invited Jenny to come and lodge with her but only for that night, after which Jenny could have it to herself for a few days. Fran planned to leave on Sunday afternoon to spend two or three days in nearby St Gervais visiting family. Her cousin was coming to pick her up then. She had said she couldn't be bothered to take the tent down just to put it back up again later, so she had booked it right through. This attitude was at variance with what was prevalent among people here, in Jenny's experience. Most alpinists would take all steps they could to minimise camping fees. She had mentioned that Watermark and Wacko would soon be joining her there, but Fran had said to let them help themselves as well, if Jenny was happy. Basically, they would be evicted as soon as Fran herself returned, but they could make themselves at home until then, and Jenny could stay on as long as she wished.

This was very welcome, saving them the effort and expense of pitching additional tents, at least for now, but of course, Jenny said she would pay for their period of use. There would be daily charges per tent, per person and per vehicle, so the rates would vary slightly from day to day. This was what M. Ravanel—and his large dog—were good at researching early each morning.

Tré-le-Champ Wedding

And so, after their second coffees, Fran had accompanied Jenny to the chalet to check the place out and help her collect her gear, which they'd then simply dumped in the vestibule of Fran's tent. This accomplished, they had set off up the valley again. A note left for Michel gave a brief explanation, concluding, "Many thanks and see you Sunday." Jenny had thought it was best just to write it in English.

Now, just coming into Tré-le-Champ, they came upon a procession for what was obviously a wedding. Without the need to discuss it, Fran and Jenny retreated from the path into slightly deeper shade and observed for a few moments, from a distance, taking in the details of the idyllic scene.

A violin and an accordion played quietly and hauntingly as the long procession snaked around the hamlet, seemingly involving its entire population. Certainly, there were people of all ages within it, all moving quite slowly but with a steady, relaxed gait. They were all dressed formally in their finery but apparently comfortably. There was a noticeable difference in clothing colours based on age: the older men and women were essentially in black, whereas the children were almost all in white or very light shades, with a range of possibilities for those in between. Jenny thought she could identify the groom, but the bride was not to be seen. As they processed around the old stone buildings, the grass long on either side of the unmade path, the sun picked out points of brilliant colour throughout the yellow-green grass—vivid gentians, campions, daisies and many others which Jenny could not identify.

Fran and Jenny looked at each other, smiling, and silently agreed that it was time to move on. Not long after turning their backs on the uplifting scene, they heard the violin and accordion take up a more uptempo, slightly zany air. They were both still smiling for some time afterwards, despite the effort of continuing on the steepening path, feeling pleased and privileged to have witnessed something traditional and real on their way.

Paper Chase

Before long, they walked past the Aiguilette d'Argentière, a small pinnacle often used for rock-climbing practice. The women were travelling very light, however, carrying only some water and provisions for lunch and a waterproof top each and wearing light trekking shoes. Jenny knew this walk from her first visit and it held no difficulty—except, perhaps, for a short section of ladders there, which overhung slightly towards the top. Their climbing practice would come tomorrow, when they had agreed to go climbing at the Lacs des Gaillands, a series of crags overlooking some small lakes just to the south of Chamonix—also known as the Guides' Crag.

After another half an hour or so, they had gained as much height as they intended to on this outing and they settled down on a large, flat stone to have some lunch. The views across to the other side of the valley were magnificent, with the principal glacier, the Mer de Glace, snaking its slow way down through sensational, jagged peaks. And behind it, easily discernible and very impressive, was the pointed fang of the Dent du Géant—the Giant's Tooth. They were in no hurry and relaxed there for a further half hour, eating, chatting, and enjoying the warmth of the sunshine whilst not having to toil against gravity in it. Of course, they also admired (and photographed) the magnificent views.

It was obviously much easier on the way down, although a little tiring on the knees on the steeper sections. They took a variation from the path Jenny had followed previously and it brought them down slightly more directly into Argentière itself. The walk would have been about 8 km overall, with nearly 1,000 m of height gain—just the thing for a rest day.

CHAPTER 27

HOW A HUNTER OBTAINED MONEY FROM HIS FRIENDS, THE LEOPARD, GOAT, BUSH CAT AND COCK, AND HOW HE GOT OUT OF REPAYING THEM

Many years ago, there was a Calabar hunter called Effiong who lived in the bush, killed plenty of animals and made much money. Everyone in the country knew him. One of his best friends was a man called Okun, who lived near him. Effiong was very extravagant and spent much money on eating and drinking with everyone until, at last, he became quite poor, so he had to go out hunting again. But now his good luck seemed to have deserted him, for—although he worked hard and hunted day and night—he could not succeed in killing anything. One day, as he was very hungry, he went to his friend Okun and borrowed 200 rods from him. Effiong told Okun to come to his house on a certain day to get his money and he told him to bring his loaded gun with him.

Now, some time before this, Effiong had made friends with a leopard and a bush cat, whom he had met in the forest whilst on one of his hunting expeditions. He had also made friends with a goat and a cock at a farm where he had stayed for the night.

Paper Chase

Though Effiong had borrowed the money from Okun, he could not think how he was to repay it on the day he had promised. At last, however, he thought of a plan. On the next day, he went to his friend the leopard and asked him to lend him 200 rods, promising to return the amount to him on the same day as he had promised to pay Okun. He also told the leopard that, if he was absent when the leopard came for his money, the leopard could kill anything he saw in the house and eat it. The leopard was then to wait until the hunter arrived, when he would pay him the money. To this, the leopard agreed.

The hunter then went to his friend the goat and borrowed 200 rods from him in the same way. Effiong also went to his friends the bush cat and the cock and borrowed 200 rods from each of them on the same conditions. He told each one of them that, if he was absent when they arrived, they could kill and eat anything they found about the place.

When the appointed day arrived, the hunter spread some corn on the ground and then went away and left the house deserted. Very early in the morning, soon after he had begun to crow, the cock remembered what the hunter had told him and walked over to the hunter's house, but he found no one there. On looking around, however, he saw some corn on the ground and, being hungry, he commenced to eat.

About this time the bush cat also arrived and, not finding the hunter at home, he too looked about. Very soon, he espied the cock, who was busy picking up the grains of corn. So, the bush cat went up very softly behind, pounced on the cock, killed him at once and began to eat him.

By this time, the goat had come for his money. Not finding his friend, he walked about until he came upon the bush cat, who was so intent upon his meal of the cock that he did not notice the goat approaching. The goat, being in rather a bad temper at not getting his money, at once charged at the bush cat and knocked him over, butting him with his horns. This the bush cat did not like at all, but he was not big enough to fight the goat. So, he picked up the remains of the cock and ran off with it to the bush. And so he lost his money, as he did not await the arrival of the hunter.

The goat was thus left master of the situation and started bleating. This noise attracted the attention of the leopard, who was on his way to receive payment from the hunter. As he got nearer, the smell of goat became very strong. Being hungry because he had not eaten anything for some time, he approached the goat very carefully. Not seeing anyone about, he stalked the goat and got nearer and nearer until he was within springing distance. The goat, in the meantime, was grazing quietly, quite unsuspicious of any danger, as he was in the compound of his friend the hunter. Now and then, he would say, "Ba!" but most of the time he was busy eating the young grass and picking up the leaves that had fallen from a tree of which he was very fond. Suddenly, the leopard sprang at the goat and brought him down with one crunch at the neck. The goat was dead almost at once and the leopard started on his meal.

It was now about eight o'clock in the morning and Okun, the hunter's friend, having had his early-morning meal, went out with his gun to receive repayment of the 200 rods he had lent to the hunter. When he got close to the house, he heard a crunching sound and, being a hunter himself, he approached very cautiously. Looking over the fence, he saw the leopard, only a few yards off, busily engaged in eating the goat. He took careful aim at the leopard and fired, whereupon the leopard rolled over dead.

The death of the leopard meant that four of the hunter's creditors were now disposed of, as the bush cat had killed the cock, the goat had driven the bush cat away (thus causing him to forfeit his claim) and the goat, in his turn, had been killed by the leopard, who had just been slain by Okun. This meant a savings of 800 rods to Effiong, but he was not content with this. Directly after he heard the report of the gun, he ran out from where he had been hiding all the time and found the leopard lying dead with Okun standing over it. In very strong language, Effiong began to upbraid his friend. He asked him why he had killed his old

Paper Chase

friend the leopard, saying that nothing would satisfy him but that he should report the whole matter to the king, who would no doubt deal with Okun as he thought fit. When Effiong said this, Okun was frightened and begged him not to say anything more about the matter, as the king would be angry, but the hunter was obdurate and refused to listen to him.

At last, Okun said, "If you will allow the whole thing to drop and will say no more about it, I will make you a present of the two hundred rods you borrowed from me."

This was just what Effiong wanted, but still he did not give in at once. Eventually, however, he agreed and told Okun he might go and that he would bury the body of his friend the leopard.

Once Okun had gone, instead of burying the body, Effiong dragged it inside the house and skinned it very carefully. The skin he put out to dry in the sun, covering it with wood ash, and the body he ate. When the skin was well cured, the hunter took it to a distant market, where he sold it for much money.

And now, whenever a bush cat sees a cock, he always kills it and does so by right, as he takes the cock in partial payment of the 200 rods which the hunter never paid him.

MORAL: Never lend money to people, because—if they cannot pay it back—they will try to kill you or get rid of you in some way, either by poison or by setting bad Jujus for you.

CHAPTER
28

RESTING IN CHAMONIX

dimanche, 4 août 1996, 11:40

As on the Grépon, two days earlier, Fran and Jenny had worked well together in their climbing at the Lacs des Gaillands. It was another glorious day and they had both climbed well. The high pressure was due to last another two to three days. They had moved gradually further up and to the left as they had picked one short route after another, again taking turns of leading. They had not bothered to try to locate a guidebook in order to check the grades of the climbs but had simply picked lines on sight. The routes they had climbed had generally been French grade 5c or 6a, which suited them very nicely.

Now, as they came back to their starting point to locate their rucksacks and have a well-earned drink of water, Jenny saw two familiar characters ambling up the path towards her.

"Oh my God! I wasn't expecting to see you guys so soon. Did you fly after all?" Jenny was genuinely surprised.

"No!" Wacko replied, managing to imbue the single syllable with several layers of "You're pulling my leg."

"We've done over two thousand miles in that van in the past ... two weeks—less, even—and it only broke down once," Watermark explained, indicating a blue Citroën van in the car park

Paper Chase

below them. (There was a typical Wacko story about that van, as Jenny later discovered.)

"That's only because of your driving," Wacko said, indignant on behalf of the van. "You should drive at a reasonable speed, like I do, and slipstream lorries whenever you can. You use twice as much fuel as me, you do, and put much more strain on everything."

"You really are like an old married couple, you two, but you're here now, which is the main thing," Jenny said, trying to prevent more bickering, before quickly pointing out the introductions. "Fran, Simon and Mark; Simon and Mark, Fran. Have you two checked into a campsite yet?"

"No, we should just park up in the woods and save money." Simon was trying to be frugal again.

Before Mark could argue with him, Jenny cut in, "Good, because I have an even better offer for you—one neither of you can complain about. Come on!"

"Where are we off to?" Simon wondered.

"We're going to the pool to cool off," Jenny informed them.

"I can't, Jenny," Mark said, not seeming too disappointed, "but I'll take a rain cheque. My wing's in the van and I've got a date with the Brévent." Mark was a keen paraglider and Le Brévent directly above them was a popular—and spectacular—venue for it. "If I stay down here, I'll only fall asleep. We've been driving for millennia."

Actually, given his present financial predicament, Mark had been more than happy to travel the long way and to share the costs. He was certainly more than happy to be back in the Alps.

Three, four more strokes and she reached the tiled wall. Jenny burst back above the surface and gulped in some air. She pushed away from the edge and moved back up the pool with a languid breaststroke, on top of the water this time. The sun beat down and the light and reflections were intense, but it was glorious to relax in the water. And where else could you do so whilst gazing up at the mesmerising array of rocky peaks that was the Chamonix Aiguilles, now sharpened in the early-afternoon sun and looking more tempting than ever. It was almost unbelievable that she had been up there, in that other world, so recently.

Actually, Jenny thought, there were two restaurants she knew where you could not only swim like this but also have a cold beer or a gin and tonic on the side of the pool and a lovely Greek salad or steak-frites on the terrace to follow—Wild Wallabies in Chamonix and Le Yéti in Argentière were popular for obvious reasons. But the views were not as good as they were here. This was the place for a rest day.

The pool area was busy, with as many people around it as in it, sunbathing, relaxing on the rounded concrete surrounds or—mostly the Antipodean contingent—juggling. The flying, coloured balls were impressive enough, but one girl from Melbourne was using long-necked silver skittles, which gleamed in the sunlight as they returned obediently to her hands. Juggling always seemed to be popular at the side of the pool and the pool was always a popular haunt for rest days, especially in weather like this.

And talking of looking tempting, Jenny approved of the rule which banned males wearing shorts in the pool. Swimming trunks were de rigueur for anyone who wanted to swim. Those who were not equipped could buy them (or even hire them) from the reception desk. Jenny felt the effect was no bad thing.

Having swum and generally played in the water for a good while, Jenny's group decided to go out into the gardens and have a late lunch of the bread, cheese, fruit and other things they had brought. Watermark had gone flying, of course, but Wacko was there. So was Fran, her recent climbing companion. Monika, the lovely Slovenian girl from the campsite, had been around but seemed to have gone. The pool complex was enclosed by a high, whitewashed wall with only one way in and out. The gardens were quite extensive but separated from the pools and their immediate environs. You had to be in one sector or the other.

Paper Chase

Some of the young lads from North London were picnicking nearby and within earshot.

"So, what's up? The Bill were crawling all over the queues at the Midi Freak—probably the others too—and those roadblocks ... they're leapfrogging them in. The top one's at the car park in Argentière, just above the *marché*." ("Téléphérique" just became "freak" to many of the Brits.)

Something was afoot. The gossip was rife. A murderer, they said. Drug traffickers, others were sure.

Having eaten what they had brought, Jenny and her companions were reclining on the grass and enjoying the sunshine. As she tried to absorb the gossip which was flying around, Jenny lay back and gazed up at the paragliders, looking like butterflies in the sky. They circled the Brévent with wings in bright colours, some gradually getting larger as they lost height. The Brévent, on the Aiguilles Rouges side of the valley, opposite to the main peaks, was always very popular for paragliders, with a high télécabine—at 2,525 m—and excellent thermals. Watermark, she knew, was up there somewhere.

From a troubled frown, Jenny's face suddenly lit up and she sat up abruptly. "Wacko, did that prat take his cell phone with him?"

"Postmark? Yes, I'm surprised he hasn't been on yet."

He was sometimes Watermark, sometimes Postmark, the latter dating back to a holiday job long ago. Instinctively, they all now looked up, peering at the circling wings and looking for pink with a single lime-green diagonal. No one could see Mark's wing.

Jenny's phone lit up as she pressed MEM—M—FIND and then green. Mark's name flashed up and he answered on the second ring.

"Hey, Jen, it's great up here!" he shouted before she had a chance to speak.

She questioned him.

"Yes, I've been watching them. I can't see the top of the valley, but they're leapfrogging up the valley from the bottom. They're trying to pen someone in. They were all over us at the chairlift."

"Thanks. Happy landings!"

"Yeeeeeee-hoooooo!" was Mark's light-hearted response.

No way out—a narrowing net on the roads, checks at the téléphériques, the rail stations and the Tunnel. Who knew what was happening on the Italian side. This could *not* be for her! Still, get away. Get some gear, some food. Go down to Les Bois and up the Mer de Glace. Two days over the mountains to anywhere—Italy, Switzerland, or elsewhere in France. She could do it. Could she get the gear?

Ping! The light bulb was above her head again

"Monika—you're going back to the site?"

With the light bulb had come her Slovenian friend, who had left them a while ago but had obviously been chatting to someone. The Fates were smiling on her, Jenny thought—at least, maybe Lachesis was. She wasn't sure she wanted Atropos smiling in her direction.

"Yes, you wanna leeft?"

Monika had exchanged a few words with the English lads in passing but had clearly been heading for the exit when Jenny had hailed her. Now, they continued together in that direction, out of earshot of the lads.

"No, but you must do me a big favour, OK? Get my harness, a rope, torch, stove, sleeping bag, bed mat—what else?—Gore-Tex jacket, Sigg bottle, axe, crampons, boots and socks. And anything else I might want for a couple of days up the hill—some clothes. Stuff them all in my big green-and-black rucksack and put them somewhere. Put them in the boot of your car … or in the storeroom next to the laundry. That's good. If anyone asks, I went off this morning up the Argentière glacier. I was with an American guy called Rick—you'd never seen him before—and we had big rucksacks. When you asked what we were going to do, I said the Dolent first of all, North Ridge."

Mont Dolent presented an imposing slope of snow and ice on its left flank when looking up the Argentière glacier. A substantial mountain in its own right, its main claim to fame was that it was

Paper Chase

the meeting place of the borders of France, Italy and Switzerland. Jenny had always fancied climbing it by the North Ridge.

"Where are you going?"

"Don't worry. It's OK. I'll be back in a day or two. Can you do that as soon as you get back to the campsite, please?"

"OK. I didn't know you were a bit mad, but I'll do it. Have a good climb with 'Rick'."

Just before leaving, Jenny returned for a brief word with the others.

"Chance of a good route—got to take it! Don't wait up."

And she was off.

CHAPTER

29

VICTOR DE CLERCQ

dimanche, 4 août 1996, 14:30

Jenny strolled out of the pool reception building, her long legs brown in the sun beneath her yellow swimsuit. Her hair was matted and chaotic, dark with the water at the ends and bleached by the sun on top. Wrapped in her towel were her T-shirt, shorts, wallet (with passport) and mobile phone. As she walked behind the pool complex towards the river, she stuffed these into a polythene bag, which she had obtained from the stroppy, uncomprehending woman in the entry kiosk. (All the woman had to do was sell one T-shirt without a bag.) She stopped to tie the neck of the bag with the lace from her small rucksack—goose-necking it as though the contents were toxic—and then dropped everything back into the rucksack, which she fastened up and slung over one shoulder as she continued over the grassy slope to her right.

"Est-ce que Victor est à la maison?"

"Oui, il vient du rivier maintenant. Qui demande?"

"Jenny!" she heard, distinctive not only because of the voice but because of the modified sounds—the softened J and sharpened Y (zhi-nee). Victor beamed at her, half out of his wetsuit, yellow helmet and gloves in hand. "Comment ça va?"

"Bien, Victor, bien"—one, two, three kisses—"mais il faut qu'on lui dépêche."

Paper Chase

"¿Que passo?" he joked.

"I need to go down the river—now!" She lowered her voice as she switched to English. He spent most of the day speaking English, she knew. "If you can lend me some gear, I'll leave it on that shingle bank at the bottom."

He looked confused.

"You remember. Where the Brazilian girl with the big nipples got cold feet."

Victor laughed out loud.

A year ago, they had met when Victor had led Jenny downriver as one of a party of novices. To *hydroglisse* downriver was much more fun and much less tame than mere white-water rafting. This was running white water with only a pair of flippers and a plastic float.

At the end of the first run, the Brazilian girl had pulled out in tears. Her feet had been painfully cold in the tight flippers and, when she had unzipped her wetsuit, her nipples had looked so painfully swollen, stretching her thin swimsuit (perhaps permanently), that they were difficult to look at. They were also difficult *not* to look at, for the same reason.

Victor had been more attentive to Jenny than to his other students. Later, they had gone out a few times—dinner, a film about glaciers, nothing serious, despite his best efforts. They had also done one long run down the river, just the two of them. Now she wanted to go five kilometres downstream by herself and dump the gear. Why? He ran a hand through his bleached curls and raised an eyebrow demandingly. She could see his torso through his flapping wetsuit, thin as a rake but perfectly muscled and bronzed.

"Look, an ex-boyfriend's looking for me. He's a real psychopath …"

"I don't believe you. Porkies!" he opined and strode into the gear room. He knew that she would recall how he had found that kind of rhyming slang, to which she had inadvertently introduced him, idiotic and yet fascinating. He returned with a wetsuit and accessories, tossing them to Jenny as he collected two floats from the stack.

"Tu vas me dire en route, hein?"

CHAPTER 30

VENDETTA

Sunday, 4 August 1996, 13:40

He was sure it was the police who had been speaking to Field that day and with whom Field had left the building. Yet there he had been, later in the week, going about his tawdry business as bold as brass. Had he not provided them with enough damning evidence to charge the bastard? Surely he had.

It was bad enough that Field was working with a criminal—OK, with a fellow criminal—to provide the loans. These were loans that charged high rates of interest and were provided to people who couldn't afford to repay them. He had been able to access some of the files and the official version was that loans would be provided only to those in employment. That was a bad joke. People with no assets and no work could still get loans but couldn't repay them. They could be bullied and threatened, though, and cajoled into other nefarious activity.

Yes, that alone was bad enough, but now it turned out that Field was stealing money from his own company.

He would bring the bastard down, one way or another.

CHAPTER
31

HYDROGLISSE

dimanche, 4 août 1996, 14:45

Jenny revelled in the feeling of the cool, milky water. Even having had the wetsuit on for only five minutes to walk down to the next bridge, in the thirty-five-degree heat, it was a delight to get into the cool at the edge of the river. They got their flippers on and moved into the flow to get underway. It felt quite familiar to Jenny and she still had control of her speed and direction—subject to a certain minimum and a certain leeway. Victor knew how experienced she was but was still the guide and was, of course, massively more experienced than she was. He gave the odd hand signal as they went along.

In a normal, commercial run, they would have perhaps ten paying customers. Victor may lead the way, but more often one of his juniors would do that and he would bring up the rear. In any event, they would have a guide front and rear—one to lead the way, giving hand signals (left, right, bunch up, look out for rocks, pull in to the side and stop) that were to be repeated by the others, and one at the rear to deal with any problems.

Now, after a few minutes' travel, Victor gave the signal to pull in and stop on the left. The technique for this was to pick a protruding rock at the edge and pull in in its lee, where the water was slack.

Paper Chase

Catching Jenny's shoulder, Victor raised his voice against the noise of the river. "There is a big hole just down here." He pointed ahead. "You may remember, but something has moved and it is a big recirc now. Keep well over to the right. You stay to my right. OK?"

She nodded and gave him a thumbs up and then they were off again.

Already, Jenny had completely forgotten about the world outside and the reason for her being there. Certain surrounding details may have been visible, but the only relevant things were those which affected the flow of the water; the river commanded her full attention. In fact, this applied both ways, although for different reasons. People on shore in the town rarely paid much heed to what was whizzing down among the millions of litres of icy water.

The remainder of the run went without incident, although Jenny did whack her knee painfully on a rock just after she had seen Victor's signal to look out for rocks. In a slightly shallower section, you couldn't afford to be too extravagant with your flipper movements. Not long afterwards, while her right knee was still feeling rather stiff, Victor again gave the sign to pull in on the left. This time, Jenny was surprised to see that they were at the shingle bank which she had mentioned and that it was time to get out. Nearly thirty minutes seemed to have passed in a flash. As they got out and felt the weight of their bodies once more, Jenny felt at once fatigued and invigorated. She had almost forgotten how exhilarating and refreshing it was.

While Victor stashed her wetsuit and the floats and flippers for later collection, Jenny quickly got dried and changed back into the clothes she had sealed in her small rucksack. They scrambled up from the river area and were soon able to join a narrow road. They were in Taconnaz, she thought, just three miles down the valley from Chamonix but outside the cordon, which was the factor uppermost in her mind. After walking southward, away from the river, for a few minutes, they came upon a nice little chalet where they could order a coffee.

"You 'aven't told me yet," Victor said and sipped his espresso.

"I … Have you seen all this police activity in the valley?"

"Yes—something big, I think."

"I just had to get out."

"But this is not something about you."

"I know—well, I hope not—but I just keep feeling penned in. I feel like I'm being trapped like an animal. I don't know. I think I'm just quietly going mad."

"You are already mad. You always 'ave been. It's what I like about you so much."

"Thanks, Victor." She reached across the table and rested her hand for a moment on his arm. "I don't know what's going on, but thanks for your help."

"De rien! It is such a long time," he replied, putting on a snooty English voice, "since I have come down this river."

"Get out of here!"

"It's good to see you, Jenny, even if you are a bit mad. But where do you go now?"

"I'll just stay down here for a bit and see what happens. My next stop is that bar down the street." They could just make it out maybe 100 metres away. "They'll have a television—and a lot of gossip. Now that I'm here, it does seem crazy, but I just felt I was being pursued and hemmed in. But how will you get back now?"

This had just occurred to her. She had not planned on having company, of course, and Victor was still in his wetsuit, once again unzipped down his chest, and was barefoot. He did look quite natural and comfortable in this attire, she had to concede—and not at all unattractive.

"Jacques will come in the van." Jacques Bernard was Victor's partner in the hydroglisse business. "I beeped him before we left."

Jacques was more than ten years older than Victor and seemed to concern himself mostly with the business side of things nowadays, leaving Victor to run the active side—to run the river.

Just then, the van swung into view and Jacques climbed out. They stood and Victor looked at the empty coffee cups and himself in his wetsuit. Jenny pulled her small wallet out of the pocket of her shorts and waved it at him with a smile. Then it was *un, deux baisers*, hello to Jacques and *un, deux, trois baisers*, farewell to Victor.

"Thanks," she said. "See you soon."

"Bonjour. Une pression, s'il vous plaît."

It was just as well she wasn't dying of thirst, as the moustachioed barman took some time to tame the frisky draught lager with his plastic spatula. The *"pression"* was Stella Artois in this establishment and so it was, of course, served in a proper Stella glass. This was another thing Jenny liked about France—the drinks were always served in the correct glass, even soft drinks, such as Orangina or Coca Cola.

She had been wrong about this place, as there was no TV set. However, there was gossip. As was usual in small, local bars in France, people actually engaged with one another. Her beer, when she eventually got it, was delightfully cold and refreshing, especially after the exertions of the run down the Arve. Her obvious enjoyment of it began the conversation.

"C'est dure, hein, la vie?" A little friendly French sarcasm from the man on her left, near the far end of the bar.

"Très dure!" was her rejoinder and she had another swig to emphasise the "fact".

She did not have to think too hard about his area of employment, as he was wearing overalls that were generally white, apart from numerous paint marks, but he must have been nearing retirement age, she thought. In front of him, on the counter, were a very small glass of lager and a glass of Pastis, together with the small jug of water which he had obviously used to give the Pastis its cloudy grey-green colour, rather like the river.

"Vous êtes en vacances ici?" he asked, turning towards her to make his enquiry.

She could now make out his features more clearly, despite the gloom at his end of the bar. He had a round, slightly podgy but friendly face framed by black hair that was greying and curly. On the left side of his bulbous nose was a large spot of whitish paint.

"Oui, à Chamonix," she confirmed, no longer feeling as though everyone was a potential enemy, "mais je viens de visiter une amie là-bas." She pointed vaguely down the valley towards Les Houches to indicate the whereabouts of the friend she had just been visiting.

One of the three men seated at a table in the corner came between them then, to replenish drinks, and he asked the barman what was going on with all of the police in the valley. This was the conversation she wanted to hear.

She was pleased with her ability to join in from time to time, albeit with fairly simple interjections and sometimes having had the chance to check the phrase in her mind first of all, but more so with her ability to understand most of the more complex language of her fellow topers. After ten minutes, it was clear that the situation was now resolved, especially when their collective understanding of the facts was fully confirmed by a local lorry driver who arrived in the bar then. This man had an impressive moustache and a no-nonsense attitude. It was all over. The police had arrested several men. No one knew why, though there were many theories. That was it. It was all over.

As a result of the lorry driver's testimony and his attitude, the conversation now turned to football and the PMU, the French lottery. A few minutes later, Jenny paid for her drink and said her farewells to the barman and the company before returning, blinking, into the sunshine. Just forty-five minutes later, she was walking into Chamonix-Sud, feeling ever so slightly foolish. She had no idea what this afternoon had been about, but actually, most of it had been quite pleasant, so who cared? She was in resilient mode and went window shopping and browsing in various climbing shops as she made her way up through the town. This was not just a devil-may-care diversion, however, as she rather hoped she might meet someone who could give her a lift the rest of the way up the valley. She had just given up on this and begun the trek up the main road towards Argentière when a van pulled over. Of course, it was Watermark.

"This is good. Apart from me getting a lift up the valley, I can actually show you where your accommodation is now." As an afterthought, she added, "Oh, but what about Wacko? I left him behind at the pool."

"I wondered why you were wandering around on your own."

"It's a long story."

"Hmm. Well, all in good time? I found this on the windscreen," he said, a little sheepishly.

He handed Jenny a note which read, "Gone to campsite. Bring the van. S."

"I forgot I had the keys," Mark said. "Don't worry about Wacko, though. He's quite resilient."

This proved to be accurate. When they arrived at the campsite, Wacko was sitting in the porch of Fran's tent brewing tea.

"Hey. You found your quarters, anyway?" Jenny said.

"Yes. Thanks very much!" He did his best to look peeved for a moment but then smiled and shrugged. "Since I couldn't get into my own van, I thought I'd turn up at the site and see what happened. I only had what was in my rucksack. Monika showed me what was what, but this tent is just about abandoned. No one at home."

"No, Fran's gone down the valley for a few days, and my ... well, most of my stuff is stashed in the room over there." She pointed vaguely to the laundry and *salle communale*. "Anyway, look, we've got this tent for the next couple of days, so there's no point in pitching anything else for now. When Fran gets back, you guys will be kicked out, so that would be the time to get some other tentage out. She just said she couldn't be bothered taking it down, because it's a bit finicky."

"I'll take it down and claim a refund." Wacko just could not help himself.

"No, we'll live in it and pay for the privilege while we do," she corrected him. "Anyway, I know I've just got back, but I've got to go up and see Michel now in Argentière. You know, Michel Louison?"

"Oh, la-di-da!" Wacko said, seeming to know who she meant, although Watermark looked a bit more puzzled.

"We're off up the Dent du Géant tomorrow," she said, "so we just need to make arrangements. I won't be long. Make yourselves comfortable." She turned to Wacko. "You already are!"

"I've got something for you," he retorted, "but it'll keep until you get back."

It wasn't more than an hour before she was back, but she went firstly to the laundry room, rather than the tent. She collected her rucksack, noting that Monika had done a good job and wondering how she was going to explain this to her in the morning. However, for now, she fished out a few useful things in the *salle communale*, to avoid the midges, which would be active outside at this relatively late hour. She boiled up some tomato soup, breaking up some leftover, slightly stale bread into it to boost it up a bit. She felt better for that and proceeded to carry her gear back up to the tent.

The lads were inside now but still chatting. She fished out her bedroll and sleeping bag and her small toilet bag but left the task of organising things for tomorrow until then. They didn't have to

Paper Chase

make an early start. In fact, the plan was to set off around 11 a.m., just early enough to get up to a good site for a bivouac. Early on Tuesday would be the time for the actual climb.

"Yes, I don't know if you want any of this stuff at the moment," Simon began without preamble, "but you may as well have it, as we may have gone up the hill by the time you get back."

He passed her some papers in a zipped plastic wallet. On top, she could see a few lined A4 sheets adorned with Simon's inimitable handwriting. It was spidery but also very legible. She knew from experience that she would have to imagine his voice as she read it, as he tended to write as he would speak, which could be rather idiosyncratically. It was clear that there was also a thicker file—a cardboard folder—behind this.

"Thanks, that's great!"

"I was able to find out quite a bit and I hope it's going to be helpful to you." He seemed a bit nervous about continuing. "There's also some information from Cameron Field in there."

"What?"

"Oh, he doesn't know about it. It's just that his file sort of fell out of the cabinet while we were passing."

After giving him the expected few minutes of scolding, Jenny began to cool down a little, especially when she heard that it was John Wade they had seen and not Cameron.

"I talked him into going in," Mark confessed in his friend's defence, "to talk about new business and have a snoop around, although I didn't expect him to swipe the whole file."

"It was the easiest way. It's just been misfiled, as far as they are concerned. I just picked it up when this guy"—he pointed to John Wade's card, which had come out in evidence earlier and still lay on the groundsheet—"left us to go back to his own desk for something. He kept trying to make out that he was going somewhere else so that we'd think we were in his office, rather than the boss man's, I think. He was a bit of a lightweight. At least now you can see whatever Mr Field has in his personal file about this woman."

Jenny had to concede, at least to herself, that this may actually be quite helpful. However, she would never have sanctioned their actions, for their good or her own or just for the sake of common decency. She had the good grace to thank them for their efforts, though, saying she should have a chance to review the papers in the morning but not now. It was time to rest.

CHAPTER
32

IGBINEDION?

lundi, 5 août 1996, 08:00

Jenny lit the stove and, while the water was boiling, she unpacked all the things which Monika had kindly packed for her. She really did not have to make very many adjustments to the gear which had been packed for her fictitious trip to Mont Dolent with "Rick", but she left the stuff strewn around at her feet for a later check and pack. Meanwhile she had some welcome coffee and fresh bread—she had already walked into Argentière this morning to buy it—with strawberry jam and honey. *Miel de savoie! (Mmm!)*

She had also bought two delicious, buttery croissants, but they were still in their paper bag, the corners of which had been expertly twisted by the *boulanger-pâtissier*. They were for Monika.

The lads were still asleep, at least one of them busy driving his pigs to the market. It was still chilly as she watched the sun approach from below, as usual.

Jenny poured a second cup of coffee and unzipped Simon's plastic wallet. Leaving the unmarked cardboard folder inside for now, she pulled out the handwritten sheets and began her perusal. *How did he do this?* she wondered.

Igbinedion?

> *Adefolake ("Ade") Igbinedion*
>
> *Dob 27/10/56 — so, she's currently 39 years old.*
>
> *Lives in South London — Morden — don't know exactly where.*
>
> *Married 11/9/87. Divorced 1989.*
>
> *Has a young son. Poplar Primary School, Morden.*
>
> *Independent sales agent for Morgan Field Associates. Sells life assurance policies for "critical illnesses" — cancer, stroke, AIDS, all that.*
>
> *Special note: contact through Managing Director C W Field only!*
>
> *BUT, she is also a solicitor. Qualified.*
>
> *She is a PARTNER in a firm called Muazu and Partners.*
>
> *Muazu and Partners — Raynes Park — Coombe Lane*
>
> *Specialising in family law, probate, property disputes, housing claims, personal injury.*

There were some other details, which were becoming less and less clear and relevant, but she just wondered how he did it. Then again, how did one get hold of Cameron Field's personal file on this matter? *(Hmm!)* To this, she now turned her attenti0n.

She extricated it from the plastic wallet with difficulty and the first thing she looked at, because it had fallen out in the process, was a slim volume entitled *Folk Stories from Southern Nigeria*, by Elphinstone Dayrell. This was not in pristine condition — it was very old and appeared to be well thumbed. Written on the half-title, in what she was sure was Cameron's hand, was "Akwa

Paper Chase

Akpa". More faintly, in a very different hand, she could make out, "To Michael—best regards. ED."

Opening the folder, she found some correspondence, which seemed to be of little importance. A copy of a letter from Field caught her eye. In it, he gave the instruction to contact the office only through him, as Wacko had reported. There was a list stapled to the left side of the folder. This was not entirely up to date, she knew from her own research, but it gave details of the policies which had come from this source. There were some calculations, in pencil, of the various amounts involved—policies, premiums, commissions and so on. She went through the body of the file a little more carefully, making sure she had seen everything. She was thinking there was really nothing much more there when she found something which really captured her attention.

It was a financial report of some kind written in small print on both sides of eight or nine sheets, stapled together. It was not clearly titled, but there was no doubt what it was.

From the declarations of interest made by all of the Morgan Field directors, which she had discovered in the higher-level background material from Mike Thomas, she knew that Cameron Field had an interest in a business called J-Cash Services, run by Jerram. She had seen the file marked "JERRAM" in his office when he had taken "IGBIN" out. What she now held in her hand was a list of loans and the financial ins and outs around them that had clearly been mistakenly filed in the folder in front of the one intended.

This listing had certainly not been prepared by an accountant, but she could see what was going on. The most recent month included was April of that year. The initial amount of capital set aside was £200,000. From that amount, new loans (of which there were many, recorded with no names, just reference numbers) and defaults (of which there were none to date) were deducted each month. Added to the total each month were redeemed loans (not quite as many, but building up) and the monthly premium.

Igbinedion?

This premium was a flat amount plus a percentage applied to the value of new loans and a higher percentage of the previous loans which were still ongoing.

So far, the effect had been that this fund had taken an initial hit but had then begun to recover slightly after month four, as the business began to become established. Leaving everything else to one side, it seemed that Cameron Field was the one who was taking the risks here, as he appeared to have been the one to set aside the initial amount of capital. He did this for someone else's business? More importantly, she felt, where was this report coming from? Surely it could be no more than a statement from J-Cash—that is, from Jerram to Field—either accompanied by a payment or by a request for a payment. At what point would Cameron Field send auditors to check Jerram's accounts? (A rhetorical question, she felt sure.)

One item in all the finely printed figures had stopped her in her tracks for a moment or two. It stood out because it was much larger than almost all of the others and had an asterisk alongside it with a footnote which said "over twenty-four months". Of course, the amount was £3,500. She was certainly concerned for her father, but he was probably right in saying that the arrangement would run its course, in his case, without any problems. Having seen these papers, though, she was also concerned for Cameron Field. In the same sort of way as her father, she felt he probably had no real idea of the kind of business in which he had become involved. She wondered just how closely this fairly plausible financial statement matched up with the actual arrangements on the ground.

There were signs of life from inside the tent now and, eventually, a couple of bleary-eyed lads emerged, looking for coffee. Anticipating this, she had put more water on. Given the power of Wacko's MSR stove and the time it had taken them to emerge, it was nearly on the boil.

"Good afternoon!" she said.

Paper Chase

Caveman noises.

"I've been reading your file, Simon. It was very interesting indeed but mainly for reasons I don't think you could have anticipated. So, I still don't really approve—certainly not of what the pair of you got up to in Edinburgh—but I may need to buy you a beer when I get back from my mountain, in any case."

CHAPTER

33

BIVOUAC

mardi, 6 août 1996, 05:45

His caress was so tender as he pushed her hair gently back from her face. Jenny was so hot and sweaty, but it didn't seem to matter. Although their lovemaking was over (for now at least), his attention was still focussed only on her. His hand stroked her arm and she felt the warmth of those cold-blue eyes as … he rose up and stood facing outward, one foot in France and one in England. He shaded his eyes from the westering sun and peered over towards Tierra del Fuego, spotting a rope of three climbers on the Central Tower of Paine, the original Bonington route. Then he turned to her and snapped his fingers. What did it mean? Did he want her to follow him? Was he displeased? Without looking back, he stepped casually into Africa and then the Middle East before taking three steps eastward and sitting cross-legged beneath the high Himalayas. The spiral was transparent and the … the … she was confused. If it … she was unsure where she was or what was going on, but she was aware that her nose hurt and that a biting wind was troubling other parts of her as well.

"Good morning."

Those knowing eyes were slightly clenched against the wind. She was not sure whether to feel loved or betrayed. He sat cross-legged, presiding over the stove, the little Markill Stormy, which

Paper Chase

was his pride and joy. The top pan was slightly raised and the freshly-scooped snow could be seen protruding.

"Are you all right?" He was suddenly concerned.

She grappled with the unfamiliar reality and frowned stupidly. She was trying to pull herself back from some far-off corner of her consciousness; he was wondering if she was suffering from the *mal de montagne* and was about to throw up.

"It's OK, I was …" dreaming.

She gradually returned to the world of the living—even though most life would be only temporary here—and began to recognise her surroundings. Only once before could she recall having experienced such disorientation when emerging from sleep. Sometimes, she hardly slept at all on a bivouac but still felt refreshed and recharged for the few hours' rest.

"You are OK?"

"Yes, I'm fine, really. I just … I must have woken up suddenly. I couldn't work out where I was or when it was or what was supposed to be happening. I didn't seem to have any recollection of anything for a moment."

"I thought you were unwell. The AMS."

Acute mountain sickness, known in French simply as *mal de montagne*, was so much more common than most people realised and it could have debilitating consequences: serious and degenerative, if not dealt with. Without proper acclimatisation—which varies from person to person—anyone, whether a green rookie or the most experienced high-altitude mountaineer, could quickly fall into difficulty. A more experienced player would probably recognise the symptoms quickly enough and treat them, the treatment being descent. The physiological changes which the body must make to be able to survive at reduced oxygen levels are not to be underestimated.

However, Jenny was well-enough acclimatised and was suffering none of these problems. She was nibbling on an oatcake now and feeling much more normal, but she had to pull back from caressing Michel's arm as he checked the warming water.

Although before 6 a.m., it was now fully light and the surrounding mountains had a subdued clarity, a grey hue which was at odds with their obvious orange tinge. The quality of the light was changing all the time. The one thing that appeared to be clear was that it would be a good day, at least until late afternoon, when possible thunderstorms had been forecast. But twelve hours was a long time in the mountains. Then again, twelve *years* was no time at all in such a land of geological character.

So, Michel was up and about already and Jenny was most reluctant to emerge from her sleeping bag, as usual.

"You are quite right," was the advice of the professional guide. "Stay in the warm for as long as possible. But we must drink and we must move on. Those are the two things which are most important."

"The fixed ropes are there, but you will not need to touch them," he had said and he had been right. The peak had been regarded as unclimbable in the nineteenth century, until it was eventually scaled—with massive use of artificial aid—in 1882. Now it was adorned (besmirched, Jenny thought) by huge white ropes, seven or eight centimetres in diameter, attached by means of steel hoops affixed to the rock. These apparently allowed guides to take incompetent people up the peak.

Moving up alongside these, she found the climbing to be very comfortable—technically, perhaps 5a in her terms, or French 5c at most. Actually, because it was still early and quite cold, she kept her gloves on for all but one short section. Although they were thin "sticky-windy" gloves designed to give good grip and feel as well as some wind protection and warmth, she would not normally have dreamt of wearing them for technical rock climbing. Now, she found herself above 4,000 m for the first time and she felt good.

Paper Chase

Although it looked like a single fang of rock from below, La Dent du Géant—or Il Dente del Gigante, as Fran would have called it (it did form part of the border)—actually had twin peaks. Consequently, a short climb down, a traverse and a further climb were required to achieve its highest point. After a brief period of mutual congratulation, rest and photography, they set off for the descent. They could already see at least two guided parties about to commence the climb.

They had left their sleeping and cooking gear in Jenny's rucksack, at the bottom of the climb—actually, at the spot where they had bivouacked at the Salle à Manger—confident that they would not be benighted on a known (to Michel) mountain after such an early start. Initially, Michel had been concerned about not carrying a tent up, but Jenny had assured him that she was quite happy in a bivouac bag with her warm sleeping bag inside it. At over 3,800 m, though, it had been colder than she had expected. However, it was a delight to travel in the mountains with Michel. He seemed to take everything in his stride and always to have the right thing to hand at the right time. He just exuded organisation and confidence. He never seemed to hurry and yet had a deceptive speed.

Now, they continued to travel light, as Michel was confident that they had ample time to traverse the spectacular Rochefort Arête, a continuation of the border between France and Italy, and still return to the téléphérique in time to descend. This really was an amazing setting, Jenny thought. The views down into Italy, which looked very green and tempting, seemed to go on forever.

They had to pass a slower party of four but did so simply by taking a line further down the slope of snow. At times, Michel took a lower line than the footprints of those who had gone before anyway, where the cornices—sections where the snow, because of the actions of the wind, formed an overhanging lip—seemed to demand it. Sections of cornices could potentially break off and collapse at any time, especially later in the season and later in the day. Clearly, you did not want to be standing on this lip when it collapsed. However, when a cornice collapses, the fracture line is not at the apex of the ridge below but rather further down, on the opposite side. The need to take a lower line on a corniced ridge is often underestimated. If a ridge has been traversed by a line which is not below the natural fracture line, that very line of footprints may, in the case of a collapse, turn out to become a fracture line, like the perforations on a roll of toilet paper.

This was a complex ridge that took an element of caution, but it was also popular. When they scrambled up the Aiguille de Rochefort at its centre—roughly halfway from their starting point to the Dôme de Rochefort beyond—they could see that there were four parties already on the next section of the ridge. There were a total of thirteen people, with two parties moving westward and two parties eastward. It was not a crowd Michel wanted to get into on purpose. Immediately, he proposed that their best course was now to return. They had experienced the best of the ridge and it was, in any case, a route where they would have to turn around and retrace their steps at some point.

There was no way Jenny would have disagreed with Michel in a matter such as this, but she did fully agree in any case. Mountaineering was more about the quality of the experience than being able to tick off a random high point. In any event, she had just achieved her second-ever 4,000 m summit. Although the Dôme de Rochefort was higher, at 4015 m, the Aiguille de Rochefort, on which they stood, was 4,001 m.

They retraced their path along the ridge, passing the slow party once more. This group of four was still trudging outward and seemed to have advanced very little since they had last met. Collecting their overnight gear from the Salle à Manger—nothing more than a flattish area, which made it popular for bivouacs or for some lunch—they continued down and then crossed the "plain" of the upper Glacier du Géant. This was a comparatively flat expanse shaped like a large basin. It was relatively safe, but they still had to be on the lookout for crevasses. A final upward slope saw them return to the téléphérique station at Helbronner. This

Paper Chase

led directly down to Courmayeur, Italy's equivalent of Chamonix, but also back to the Aiguille du Midi, above Chamonix, by the most spectacular crossing of the huge, high upland of ice which was the Vallée Blanche. Jenny had now made this crossing several times, but it was still breathtaking—as, of course, were the views from the platforms of the stations at Helbronner and the Aiguille du Midi. The engineering was also astonishing and did make these views available to those who would never otherwise be able to see the wonders of this high world of rock and "royal icing".

CHAPTER 34

STRESS

Tuesday, 6 August 1996, 10:00

Dennis Wardlaw was in a bad mood and was feeling stressed. He often felt stressed and he knew that when he was stressed he tended to eat. Now, he was due to be going off on holiday soon and had been trying to lose weight, but he was gaining weight instead. This made him feel even more stressed.

Bloody computer system! He had not been the one who had picked it. They had turned his recommendation down as being too expensive. However, he was the one who had been expected to make the piece of junk work. Cameron Field, his boss, had the habit of *sounding* quite reasonable about it all, so long as any little thing which was discovered to be less than perfect was rectified yesterday (the afternoon would be OK!). Bloody Field!

Dennis had always been good at his job, but he did feel as though he was beginning to be overtaken by new developments these days. Having just turned 53, he felt old to be in a young man's discipline like IT. A young *person's* discipline, he corrected himself. Bloody women!

He never heard from his ex-wife. So long as she got the money, she kept quiet. The kids were growing up now and he saw less and less of them. In some ways, this suited him quite well, but he still felt somehow cheated and left out.

Paper Chase

He recognised that he was in a bad mood. It was time he was off to Kalogiroi to relax and recharge his batteries. This year, he was determined to move things along with Mariella. He would arrange to see her as soon as he arrived and give himself the maximum amount of time. He wondered if the local plumber had sorted out the problem in the kitchen there properly.

Most of the men in his family were tradesmen, time-served artisans, if they were not labourers, as his own father had been. He was not from a family of professionals or office workers, but—in computers and computing—he had just found something he could understand and was good at. It happened at the right time for him. So why could he not just be called "IT director", as many of his counterparts in other organisations were? He could be a titular director without needing to hold equity. But, oh no. "Head of IT" was the correct term for his job. Bloody Morgan Field. And now this auditor was snooping around, pestering him and Field seemed to be on his case more than ever.

He went to get a sandwich.

CHAPTER 35

EPIPHANY

mercredi, 7 août 1996, 10:15

Jenny was back in the *Office de Haute Montagne*. She and Michel had celebrated with a pizza the previous evening, after their return from the mountains. They had washed it down with a glass or two of wine, but that was after Jenny had drunk some water, two mugs of tea, a small beer and most of a large bottle of Orangina on her immediate return to the valley. There seemed to be no end to her thirst. She knew it had not been an expedition worthy of celebration for Michel, but she really appreciated his taking her out, especially when he was supposed to be having a break and when he would normally have charged a good fee for a trip such as that. It was something of a busman's holiday for him but was very much appreciated by her. He had also made a convincing case that he was really pleased to make the trip and happy to have had the opportunity, citing the enjoyment he still derives from taking others to experience new places and thresholds.

She had taken the opportunity of a lift into Chamonix with Monika, who was leaving now, setting off through the Tunnel du Mont Blanc for the long but pleasant crossing of Northern Italy on her way back to Ljubljana. They had exchanged addresses and good wishes and Monika had got on her way, after an affectionate hug.

Jenny felt a little sorry for Watermark and Wacko, as the weather was not now what it had been in recent days. There had been a note in the tent when she had got back saying that they had gone up to the Plan de l'Aiguille for two or three days. Their remaining gear had been stowed neatly in the porch of the tent, anticipating Fran's return. If one carried some food and bivouac gear, this was certainly an area where many different routes were accessible, but then that applied to the whole of the surrounding area, she thought with a smile. What a place! Anyway, they would be able to get some good climbing in, it was just that it would not be quite so sunny and they certainly would not stay dry the whole time. There had been a huge thunderstorm at about ten o'clock last night, but it had been short-lived. The same sort of thing was likely for today but probably slightly earlier in the evening.

Jenny was alone in the room, apart from the unobtrusive staff member, who was quietly getting on with some work behind his desk. On the table in front of her were a map and a guidebook, but these had been left behind by someone else. On this visit, she was not making uphill plans and was not seeking company or communication—and neither did she need to use the toilet.

She was simply using the place as a convenient base to sit down and try to understand her own situation. Why had she been behaving so irrationally? She scribbled on a pad, trying to analyse and understand her own psyche. Whenever her security seemed to be threatened—she went back and underlined "seemed to be"—she behaved irrationally and took flight.

That police hunt in the valley *couldn't* have been for her, but she'd gone to elaborate lengths to escape downriver—the only *unexpected* way she could see to get away. In Glasgow, she'd *stolen a car* after running away from the police. She'd had a speeding ticket before and another one wouldn't have killed her, but she'd never "broken the law" broken the law before.

Epiphany

Paranoia. Corticosteroids. These two words came, seemingly unbidden, into her mind. It felt like the light bulb above her head again, but this time she had the impression that she had lit it by the slower method of pulling a cord to operate a clicker switch.

A quick search in the pocket of her rucksack allowed her to find the second word, while a relocation to Chamonix's excellent public library, just a short walk away, and fifteen minutes of research in the medical section allowed her to link it to the first. (Actually, it took longer, but only because she'd often had to make use of the largest French-English dictionary she had ever seen to facilitate the research.)

Could it really be? The medication (apparently a glucocorticoid, part of the corticosteroid "family") she had been taking for a minor skin complaint had possible *ESPs* (*effets secondaires psychiatriques* or, in English, psychiatric side effects) which included psychosis! She had nearly completed the course but decided on the spot to take no more.

Could she work on the assumption that this—she could scarcely believe it—had been the cause of her odd behaviour and make up for it by more rational and logical action from now on? As Sir Arthur Conan Doyle had written, "When you have eliminated the impossible, whatever remains, however improbable, must be the truth."

She sighed and rubbed her hand through her hair. This was bizarre. *As my behaviour has been*, she couldn't help thinking.

"Un café et un verre de rosé, s'il vous plaît." Jenny had met Liv, the Danish woman, and agreed to go for a coffee, but Liv preferred a glass of wine. They had not met since that first day with Fran, so they were catching up on what each had been doing. They were in The Alpenstock, another traditional Chamonix cafe, and the waiter returned with their drinks in what seemed no time.

Liv and her Swedish friend, Ronja, had done a few good routes together, but the headline one had been climbing Mont Blanc via Route Major, a long and technical ascent from the south side. However easily she could enthuse about the Grépon, Jenny was pleased to have the Dent du Géant and Aiguille de Rochefort to report as well.

Liv was quite loud and expansive but very funny. They got on easily and had a very pleasant chat. It was not just Liv's easy style, however. Jenny was feeling better in herself. She had been feeling edgy, panicky at times, and concerned over how she had been acting. Now that she had discovered a possible explanation and had had a little time for it to sink in, she was feeling better than she had for some time. She felt something of her normal confidence and self-assurance had returned to her and, feeling pleased about it, she resolved to accept this explanation and move on apace.

She would bundle up what papers she had and what notes she had made—in Simon's plastic wallet, if they would all fit—and park them until she got home. Compartments. Meanwhile she was in the Alps. She was on holiday and she would get the most out of her remaining time.

They chatted about future plans and it was clear that Liv and Ronja had many future objectives, some of which sounded challenging indeed. Jenny kept the objectives she listed a little less ambitious but realised, as she set them out, that they were very genuine objectives for her. She had just a bit more than a week left after today. However, she had been here for less than a week and already had three good routes under her belt. Some people would spend a month here without achieving as much.

She was feeling positive.

She was also feeling lucky, as Liv was heading back to the campsite and had a car. Jenny was doing well—she had not had to walk the full distance between Chamonix and Argentière once so far.

Epiphany

After meeting Ronja at the campsite, Jenny went out with the other two to climb on the nearby crags at La Joux. On their return, they found that Fran had arrived back and the four of them proceeded to chat and catch up whilst combining their resources to prepare a rather tasty (but somewhat random) feast on the campsite.

While this work was ongoing, Mark and Simon returned, having cut their trip a bit short in view of the weather. They were clearly too late to contribute much to dinner, but there was plenty to go around and they were still made very welcome. In the end, they did more than enough, as Mark produced a large watermelon from the top of his bulging rucksack while Simon recovered some beers and a bottle of wine, which had been chilling for several days in the water trough with his name on them.

And of course they had a tent to erect, so they could not be expected to help with the washing up. In fact, they erected it very quickly indeed, as the first flashes and deep, threatening rumbles of a storm were followed by spaced, heavy droplets, presaging the torrent which was shortly to follow. Once inside—and only superficially wet—they were both glad of their decision to conclude their adventure on the Plan de l'Aiguille a day early. This time, the poorer weather continued, pretty much unabated, for the next two days.

CHAPTER
36

INTELLIGENCE

Friday, 9 August 1996, 11:45

Cameron Field's door was closed. Determined to make some serious progress after the events of recent days, he just wanted to get his head down, without interruptions. He had made this clear to Jean, so why was she buzzing through in the middle of the morning?

"Mr Field, I know you're busy, but I have your solicitor on the telephone and I wondered if you would like to speak to him."

I've been interrupted already, so I may as well, he thought, but said, rather more charitably, "Yes, thank you, Jean."

"Ah, Mr Field, I wanted to let you know, with a suitable caveat or two, some additional information which I have been able to glean since our last discussion. The principal caveat is really that this is not definite but rather contains an element of speculation and supposition. The secondary caveat is that I would urge you not to use any information I may give you in this connection in any direct way but rather to inform any private cogitation which you may have, or indeed any subsequent privileged discussions which you and I may have. Is that all acceptable?"

"Yes, yes, I understand."

"Very well. Very much informally and—as I say—with an element of conjecture, it appears, from discussions with certain parties within the police organisation, that the information they have has reached them through a member of your own staff. Again, I would stress that this is not definite and that, in any case, the prudent response would be simply to consider and observe, rather than taking any more direct action and certainly rather than making it known to anyone that you have any such suspicion."

"Hmm."

"Mr Field?"

"Just 'cogitating' for a moment," he said, thinking, *This is wasted on him.*

"Ah, no immediate instructions in this connection, then?"

"No, but that may well be helpful. Thanks."

The telephone call may have lasted less than five minutes, but Cameron found that it disturbed his concentration for considerably longer.

CHAPTER
37

ENVERS DES AIGUILLES

samedi, 10 août 1996, 11:30

The third day after the impromptu party dawned overcast but dry. The forecast was for another few days in which high pressure would dominate and so the plan was to get uphill and take advantage. For most, the previous two days had involved nothing much apart from reading, eating, sleeping, planning for the end of the poorer weather and watching a bit of a tennis tournament in The Office. This was not the *Office de Haute Montagne* in Chamonix but The Office Bar in Argentière. Feeling so much better, however, Jenny had also spent several peaceful hours attempting to capture (on Daler board) the idyllic mood of the wedding scene in Tré-le-Champ.

Now, by contrast, there was a flurry of activity, with bodies and gear spilling out of tents, discussions being held as to what equipment was required and additional supplies of food being purchased in the town. Michel was away in Switzerland again for a few days, but they had arranged to meet up on Friday, before Jenny departed. The plan, for Jenny and her friends, was to take the rack-and-pinion railway from Chamonix to Montenvers on the left bank of the Mer de Glace and then hike up from there to spend probably four nights in the vicinity of the Refuge de l'Envers des Aiguilles, the hut at the opposite side of the Aiguilles de Chamonix. The party was to be Jenny, Mark, Simon, and Fran, but Fran would have to descend on Tuesday to team up with her regular climbing partner from Italy. The others planned to spend Tuesday as a third day climbing and to descend on Wednesday.

Fran and Jenny intended to stay in the hut, *chez Babette*. Babette was the legendary *guardienne* of the Refuge de l'Envers des Aiguilles, or Envers Hut, regarded by many as the best hut anywhere around, if not anywhere in general. Simon and Mark planned to bivouac nearby. In fact, Simon also preferred to save the train fare by hiking up through the woods, so the others took his heavy rucksack on the train so that he could travel light on that first leg at least. They would meet up at the Montenvers station.

Simon set off much earlier but was still overtaken by the train eventually. However, it was no hardship to spend a while waiting in the station area. There were cafe/bars, souvenir shops and a general bustle of tourists, many of whom would take the cable car down to the Mer de Glace, where an ice cave was dug out of the side of the living ice with ice sculptures inside for them to explore. This was not a trip for the faint-hearted. Although the cable car took care of most of the height difference, there were still many flights of steps to descend and then ascend again. As the glacier was flowing quite quickly—imperceptibly to the eye but at a rate of about one centimetre per hour—a new ice cave was dug out each summer. A line of old, partially collapsed caves could be seen further down the glacier, spaced about eighty or ninety metres apart.

Of course, there were also mountaineers in great numbers. They came in two main types. The first type were the fresh and eager climbers, talking and laughing loudly as they made their way down the long, sloping path through the shops and towards the series of long ladders which led down to the glacier. The second type of climbers looked exhausted but happy. They were either trudging slowly up that long slope while leaning heavily on their poles, their large rucksacks bearing down on them, or else were already seated gratefully, still looking fatigued, in a terrace cafe

Paper Chase

with beers on the table and their heads inclined upward towards the magnificent views.

Not least among these views, Jenny thought, were the Petit Dru, an incredible spike of orange granite when seen from this close up, and the huge, looming bulk of the Grandes Jorasses, one of the six great north faces, which rose to a height of 4,208 m. Further right, following the skyline that was the French-Italian border, was her unseen friend the giant's tooth. The Dent du Géant, which she had seen from the train, was just out of sight from this angle.

Simon was not far behind them and they paused only to allow him to have a drink of water, fill up his bottle and shoulder his pack before joining the flow and becoming part of the first type of mountaineers.

The ladders leading down to the glacier were a real bottleneck, as they were in use for climbers returning from the glacier as well as those trying to reach it. When the four of them had reached the edge of the glacier, they donned their crampons and stepped on to the ice, gingerly at first but with quickly growing confidence.

There was no need to rope up, as the glacier was dry down at this level, meaning it was solid, blue ice, free from the covering of snow to which they were accustomed. This being the case, the crevasses were clearly visible, as well as huge and numerous, so they had only themselves to blame if they fell into one.

The crevasses were so numerous, in fact, that one had to follow a circuitous, maze-like route to progress up the glacier. This would have taken much longer but for the line of ice granules, caused by the passage of many crampons before theirs. When they had moved about two kilometres upstream—although they had walked much further—there was a large red-and-yellow painted sign on their right (the orographic left bank) showing where they should leave the ice to scramble up the loose lateral moraine in order to gain more stable ground.

The moraine was as unpleasant as ever, being loose and dusty rock, ground out and pushed along by the massive weight of the ice, but they quickly gained a good path. This was hard-packed brown mud, working its way along and up through dwarf rhododendrons and azaleas and the *myrtilles*, which were so common in French patisserie. No one was sure if they were bilberries or blueberries (or whether there was a difference), but Fran called them *mirtilli*, like the French, and Mark called them *frocken*. There were also all kinds of grasses and thistles and occasional points of bright colour from Alpine flowers, which were mostly unknown to them.

The cloud cover had broken up and the promised fine weather was clearly emerging. It was very still on this bank and becoming very hot. Simon and Mark were carrying the heavier packs, of course, including sleeping bags, stove, food and so on, and Simon had been silent and apparently thoughtful for some time.

"Everyone's boots have polished these stones," he said.

"What?" Watermark's tone implied criticism, rather than a desire to understand.

"And packed this mud down," Simon continued his own line of thought.

"Wacko, what are you on about?"

"Everyone's been up here—everyone you've ever heard of, in climbing terms, and a lot more you probably haven't. Name a mountaineer: his boots have polished these stones." It was an interesting thought.

Just then, the hut came into view high above them. It was built out on a promontory to be safe from avalanche and stone-fall. They knew the way and continued beyond it, beneath it, until there was a fork in the waymarked path with the route straight on leading to the Requin Hut and the branch to the right leading back and steeply up to their objective.

When perhaps 100 m below the hut and maybe 300 m or 400 m south of it, Wacko and Watermark began looking for likely places to bivouac. Agreeing to meet up on the terrace of the hut at about nine o'clock next morning for a leisurely start, they split into two companies. As Fran and Jenny approached the hut, a woman

Paper Chase

quickly approached them. Neither old nor young, fair hair tied up behind her head, clad in a pair of shorts and a fleece top, she moved lightly and very quickly in her soft trekking boots, pausing to exchange a brief greeting before continuing towards Mark and Simon. This was Babette and she reached them very swiftly. She came not to chase them away, as some hut proprietors might have done, but to advise them on the best and safest spots to bivouac. She regained the hut and disappeared into the kitchen just as Fran and Jenny were getting into hut slippers, having only just had time enough to shed their boots.

Two hours later, they were seated around a large table, talking several different languages and tucking into chicken noodle soup, bread, polenta, omelettes, cheese and a wonderful dessert. If Jenny spared a thought for the lads below, it was only to think, *Ha!*

CHAPTER
38

BELAYING

lundi, 12 août 1996, 10:50

Standing on a rough ledge about ten centimetres wide and a metre long, Jenny was in the shade, shivering slightly and just waiting for the sun to edge towards her. When it did, she knew she'd be too hot almost instantly, but right now she still longed for it.

The rope was running out slowly, so she knew the way ahead was difficult or unclear, or more likely both. She watched a tiny spider fall carelessly off the ledge and disappear below her. It would be fine, of course. It would spin its own lifeline or else just catch the breeze and come to rest, like a skydiver giving a timely tug on the risers for a smooth landing. A heavy animal like her, however, would have no such second chances. She rolled a tiny stone down and watched it bounce and whirl its way downward until out of sight. In a fall, she would bounce and whirl like that. Without a rope to draw tight and minimise injury, she would eventually land and—unlike the spider—have too much force and momentum to prevent her own body from breaking and rupturing, most likely (hopefully?) terminally.

She tried to pull herself away from these thoughts, but they were almost inevitable when you spent too much time static on a belay. What if Fran fell? Well, the whole purpose of Jenny's

Paper Chase

belay was to be strong enough to hold them in case of such a fall. Besides, Fran had placed three ... no, four running belays which Jenny could see and no doubt more which she could not. All of those also conspired to hold the two of them to the rock, no matter what. But still, those nagging, negative thoughts would rise to the surface, her mind thinking ahead in a kind of desperate self-preservation routine.

Surely it was good to think, "what if?" It kept you ... *grounded*, she tried not to think.

CHAPTER
39

DINNER FOR THREE

mardi, 13 août 1996, 19:55

There were others present, but this was the first time the three friends had sat down to dinner together, except on the campsite. To mark the last night of their stay around this side of the Aiguilles de Chamonix, Jenny had made a magnanimous offer.

"I said I'd buy you a beer, but I'll buy you dinner as well, my treat, though if you want to start adding copious extra beers, you're on your own!"

"That's good," had been Wacko's very gracious response. "We've run out of food anyway."

The catering did not disappoint and both Wacko and Watermark had had seconds (at least) of everything so far. Jenny had arranged for a carafe of red wine to be put on the table and it was actually rather good for 45 francs, especially with the cheese, which was now being served.

After two and a half great days of climbing, Fran had had to go down at lunchtime. They had offered to accompany her, but she'd been more than happy to make the trip by herself. They would never have crossed a snow-covered glacier singly, where you could drop into an unseen crevasse that could easily be fifty metres deep or more, but the dry glacier they had come over on the way up here was a different proposition. So, Jenny and Fran

Paper Chase

had eaten lunch together sitting on the terrace of the hut, having made their way back there, across and down the small glacier at the foot of the climb they had just completed and from which they had abseiled back down. Before they finished lunch, Wacko and Watermark had come in from their climb and joined them, so they had all said their farewells. It had not always been the two girls climbing together and the two boys climbing together—they had used all available combinations, but Wacko/Fran and Watermark/Jenny had been one of the most common.

Now, at dinner, it was nice for the three of them to sit down together, chat and be catered for, for a change. *It's more of a luxury for them than for me*, she thought, and she was glad she had made the offer. The only thing which seemed to have pleased Simon more than a free meal was when they had turned up on the terrace as arranged—actually, slightly early—on the first morning to find three lean, strong fellows laying out, counting and bagging some very serious ironmongery.

These were Michel Piola and his friends Gérard Hopfgartner and Vincent Sprungli. They were preparing to re-equip a few older, classic routes of theirs. Piola was particularly well known, as a leading exponent of modern rock routes in the mountains and as the writer of the guidebooks in common use. Jenny had the Piola guide to this area in the top pocket of her rucksack. She had been pleased to meet Michel Piola and his colleagues and had been fascinated and pleasantly surprised by their ethic of placing bolts in these routes only from the ground up, never on abseil.

Pleased she may have been, but Watermark and particularly Wacko were transfixed and had spent more than an hour chatting to the trio, meaning that her party had not even left to trek towards their first route until about 10:15 a.m.

Anyway, the wonderful dessert had been served again now—the same as before, but she had certainly not yet had time to tire of it. It was a sort of bombe made with fresh apples, cream and sponge fingers soaked in some form of liqueur and it was very fresh and tasty.

Dinner for Three

"So, we don't need to be too early tomorrow—say, about nine?" Mark was trying to sort out the planning. They intended to climb one short route in the morning, as a party of three, before gathering up their kit and heading back down the glacier.

The route, Sonam, was not too technically demanding and was just above the hut, which meant that they could reach the foot of it in fifteen or twenty minutes. It was seven pitches in length, a height gain of 200 m, with six abseils required to descend the line of the climb. Overall, even as a three, Jenny reckoned they could do it in four and a half to five hours, from the hut and back. This would allow them to have a quick bite of lunch before setting off down, with adequate time to catch the train back down to the valley. They had saved this route for the purpose.

"Nine will be fine," Jenny confirmed.

Then, with a final toast, the boys had to extricate themselves from the comfort of the hut and make their way back down to their bivouac site for their final night there. Jenny would merely have to make use of the facilities within the comfort of the hut. She would twist on a switch in the toilet which would allow the light to stay on for thirty seconds and then make her way back to her place in the cool and airy basement. Clearly, she was trusted not to steal the extra stores of foodstuffs that were down there. It certainly had more air and fewer noisy distractions than the main dormitory rooms higher up in the building.

"A good last day and a safe return!" Watermark said.

"Santé!" she replied.

CHAPTER
40

REAPPRAISAL

Thursday, 15 August 1996, 17:10

Having had a further brief dialogue with the local constabulary, this time with his solicitor present, Cameron Field had a few things on his mind. Remembering the previous discussion with his solicitor, he had been giving some consideration to the idea that a member of his staff may be trying to cause trouble. He had no illusions about the way he was regarded. He was not an all-powerful, all-providing demigod, worshipped without question by his people. He was the person in charge. He made decisions. Some of those would be popular and some would not.

He was concerned about his head of IT, Dennis Wardlaw, who had seemed to be a bit erratic lately and even more stressed than usual. However, the recent line of enquiry from the police had raised questions he would need to take up with Jerram. Their contention was that loans were being granted to almost anyone—including those without an income—whether or not they had a realistic chance of repaying and that the old bully-boy tactics were coming into play, with heavy-handed efforts being made to encourage repayment by any means.

This did not reflect the modus operandi on which they had agreed and he needed to raise this urgently with Jerram. Unfortunately, he could not get hold of the man. The July bordereau was also now late—the first time that a monthly report had been late in all the months they had been working together.

Taking all of this together, particularly his continuing dialogue with the police, who could be somewhat hostile at times, he was not at all satisfied.

CHAPTER 41

DINNER FOR TWO

vendredi, 16 août 1996, 20:45

Jenny looked out at the River Arve flowing swiftly past the window at what appeared to be about the same level as her knees under the table. She thought back to last Sunday and realised that she must have whizzed past this very window.

She had spent the day climbing with Simon. They had climbed a route called Les Lépidoptères on the lower north-western slopes of the Aiguille du Peigne. When she suggested it, she had expected him to object to paying for another trip up to the Plan de l'Aiguille, the halfway station on the Aiguille du Midi téléphérique, especially as the whole point was that the route was neither too long nor too hard and could be easily accomplished in a day. He had been quite keen, however, and it was Watermark who excused himself. (He had a troublesome knee and felt that some ibuprofen and a day's rest would do it good.) It had been a thoroughly enjoyable outing and they had been back down in the valley in good time, which had been Jenny's prerequisite.

She turned back to Michel. She had been reflecting during a brief lull in their conversation, which had been relaxed, friendly, and informative. They did seem to have an easy rapport and it was hard to remember that they had met only just over two weeks ago.

It had been an open invitation for dinner and she had thought that there might be as many as half a dozen around the table. However, Watermark and Wacko had opted out, saving their pennies. In the end, it was only Jenny and Michel. On that basis, he had suggested l'Atmosphère, here in Chamonix, whereas Argentière's TexMex may have been the more likely venue for a larger, more mixed party.

You entered l'Atmosphère, possibly the best restaurant in Chamonix, from a corner of the main square. A flight of stairs then took you down to a wonderful dining room, where you could enjoy the delights of haute cuisine as the River Arve rushed past your window. It was quite a spot and both the starters and the main courses had been excellent. That was as far as they had got, but they had been looked after well, in a way that was attentive but not fussy.

"Thank you for being so friendly to a stranger on an aeroplane."

"Mais, de rien."

"I was dealing with a lot of difficult stuff at work and I was finding it hard to switch off and relax. You helped me to do that, so thank you. Not to mention my first four-thousand-metre peak—that was fantastic!"

"Mais, oui. You always remember the first." He smiled and stared at her guilelessly. "But I will be in London—and elsewhere UK—again in a few weeks. I was returning from some lectures and signing books when we met. You think when you complete the book that is the end, but no—this is only the beginning."

"Oh, what's the book called? I'd like to get one."

"But I will give you one."

"No, you will not," she scolded. "You're in business to sell these, not to give them away. And we haven't even sorted out what I need to pay for my first few days at the chalet with you."

"OK, now I have a plan. You can buy a book, I'll make a special dedication and that's it—ç'est tout! And when I am next at the Alpine Club or somewhere, you can buy me a traditional English curry."

"OK, I'll agree to that plan on one condition: if you're writing off any fees for my accommodation for the first few days, I am paying for dinner tonight."

"Mais, non—"

"Non, pas de dispute—ç'est finale!" she said, hoping that meant what she intended it to mean.

"Vous avez choisi?" The waiter appeared to have been hovering discreetly.

"Non, trois minutes, s'il vous plaît," she replied. They had not even glanced at the dessert menus as yet, but Jenny imagined that this was the sort of place which would do a really excellent crème brûlée.

CHAPTER 42

BACK TO WORK

Monday, 19 August 1996, 08:30

"Bryony, it's Jenny. I'm only here today, but I really need to catch up with Mike about Morgan Field at some point. Does he have some time free?" With no more than a glance at her desk, she had picked up the phone as soon as she had arrived in her office.

"Oh, he's choc-a-bloc, Jennifer. Right now would be best, although he's just about to go into a meeting." She lowered her voice, conspiratorially. "I'm not even going to ask him. I'll just tell him I've told you to come up and you're on your way."

"OK, on my way right now." She put down the phone and left her office again immediately.

"Jenny, hi. Grab a seat. I really only have a minute. Did you have a good break?"

"Yes, it was just lovely!" she said, enthusiastic but as brief as possible.

"Sorry I missed you before, but you know what it's like. I did try to call you when I got back. It was on the Friday afternoon—but in fairness, I wasn't sure if I'd catch you. It was quite late in the day."

"Yes, I did ... leave a bit early."

Leaving it at that, she wondered whether the receptionist in Edinburgh would have said, "I'm afraid she isn't here at present," or "Hell, no. She hasn't been here since the start of the week." She thought the former was more likely and that it would probably have been said to Bryony anyway. Mike was clearly keen to move on in any case.

"One or two issues with the Morgan Field job, I believe?"

She explained how things stood as quickly and cogently as she could, as he listened intently.

"Erm ..." He held up a time-stopping index finger and then snapped his fingers when he remembered. "Franklin!"

Before Jenny could get any further clarification, Bryony popped her head around the open door.

"They're waiting for you in room six, Mike."

"Send them my apologies, Bryony, but tell them I will be there in a few minutes. Now, Jenny, what you were saying is exactly right, but make sure you incorporate a wording similar to the one I put into the Franklin report earlier this year. Get Bryony to give you a copy. Good luck! And well done. It's not easy when you really have to start questioning the senior people you're working with—especially if you already know them. You really seem to have kept your eye on the ball here. Let me have a copy of your final report when you get a chance. I've no doubt it will come back to me to field a few bits and pieces sooner or later. I don't need chapter and verse, but keep Bryony posted as to any really material feedback or developments. I'll keep you in the loop likewise, if I possibly can. Anyway, must go. Well done!"

In one movement, he rose, grabbed his jacket off the back of the chair, shrugged into it and left the room. Glancing around in a kind of reflex reaction, Jenny saw Bryony passing him some coloured files as she walked with him from the outer office, quietly providing him with updated information. Jenny had gathered her thoughts and made a few quick notes by the time Bryony returned.

"Bryony, the Franklin report ..."

Back at her own desk, with a borrowed copy of Franklin, she did have a quick look through everything that had landed there before trying to get on with the Morgan Field work. She also called her friend Edith and arranged to meet for lunch.

It had been an uneventful flight back home. A colleague of Michel's had been going to the airport on Saturday morning anyway, so all the farewells had been in the Valley. (Fran was still away, so Tuesday's farewell had had to suffice.) It was always slightly sad coming to the end of a trip to the mountains, but that just emphasised how good it had been to be there.

Everything had been in order when she had got home. There had been no police cars parked outside and no arrest warrants on the doormat. She had panicked a bit when she had found a letter from Lothian and Borders Police in her post but, of course, it had been regarding the recovery of her hire car. Actually, the letter had been to the owners, the hire company, and hers had been a copy for information. It had stated that the car had been found and had given details of how it could be recovered. She wondered if Loudmouth's car had also been recovered.

This reminded her of the story of Wacko's Citroën van, which had come out during their dinner in the Envers Hut. He had apparently read up on the legislation governing abandoned vehicles on the Highway. As result of this, he had claimed this abandoned Citroën van, even though he had no idea who actually owned it. He had been keeping an eye on it and, when sufficient time had passed, he had stepped in, only having to pay a small charge before being allowed to take it away.

Paper Chase

This was a typical, nutty Wacko story, where his research and pluck had got him a free van. However, there was also a typical, nutty Wacko sting in the tail. Just before leaving on his recent 2,000 mile (so far) road trip, he had received a summons alleging the theft of a motor vehicle. Apparently, the owner had eventually called to claim it and had been surprised that it had already gone—not to be crushed, but to another person who had claimed it. Before leaving, Wacko had filed a brief reply stating the basis on which he had claimed it and he still maintained that he was confident of his position. Jenny was not so sure, but then she would never risk getting on the wrong side of the law ...

By the time she had got through the layers of things on her desk, designating them as urgent, important, both or neither, had taken the Franklin report details she needed and had fielded a few urgent queries, it was already time to go and meet Edith.

"The Man with the Child in His Eyes"—as she was leaving, she realised that Kate Bush had been in her head, probably for most of the morning.

CHAPTER 43

SANDWICH LUNCH

Monday, 19 August 1996, 13:05

Edith Adebayo sat on a stool at the counter near the shopfront windows, a glass of fresh orange juice with lots of ice in her hand. Instead of drinking it, she rested it against one cheek and then the other. She also enjoyed the cool feel of it against her forehead for a moment before she took a sip. A week from Friday, she would be off on two weeks' leave and then she would have only five weeks more before she would be off on maternity leave. This was a bigger adventure than anything she had done before, but now she was feeling the oppressive late-summer heat in the city.

"Sorry I'm late," Jennifer Andrews said as she bustled in and kissed Edith in greeting. "How are you? You look great."

"I'm hot," Edith laughed. "I'm fine, though. Everything's good."

"Anyway, sorry, I was struggling to get away from people, just being back today."

"It's no problem. I've only arrived just before you." She waggled her nearly full glass in evidence.

"Do you know what you want? I can get them just now."

"Tomato and mozzarella, please, on ciabatta."

"OK, two ticks."

The four ladies of assorted ages behind the serving counter

were doing a good job of dealing with orders and keeping the queue down as customers flocked to this popular sandwich bar, some for takeaway orders and others to dine on the premises. It was not long before Jenny returned to the counter in the window, a large glass of Lilt clinking in her hand.

"How much longer do you have now, then?"

"Well, depends what you mean. The baby's due on the thirteenth of December, but I'll get back from holiday on the sixteenth of September. Then I'll only have five more weeks at work."

They continued to chat, but it was not until their sandwiches had arrived and had been half consumed that Jenny raised the issue she had wanted to discuss. Edith's parents had met in London, but had both moved there from Nigeria in the very early 1960s, just after independence. Although Edith had been born and raised in London, Jenny knew that she was fascinated by her West African roots and was knowledgeable on the subject.

"As part of an investigation I'm involved in, I came across a book of old Nigerian folk tales." Jenny fished the book out and laid it on the counter.

"Oh, I think I might have seen that one before. I'll know a lot of the tales anyway." Edith picked it up and glanced down the index. "Yes, I know these. A lot of them are a bit weird—and quite harsh and uncompromising too. But then look at the collection of standard Northern European tales from the Brothers Grimm."

"Yes, I suppose so. Do you know much about Nigerian names? I don't suppose it matters, really—a name's just a name, isn't it?"

"Well, a bit. It's a big subject, but Nigerian names are a lot more like the way people think about American Indian names. You know, 'Dances with Wolves', 'Stands with a Fist'—that sort of thing. It's complicated, though, because there are several different naming styles, Yoruba and Igbo and also Muslim names, but they all cross over a bit as well. There's a fondness—I think especially Yoruba—for shortening names. A lot of the names are circumstantial, meaning the child is supposedly a recently deceased adult who has come back or the second born of twins or the name will just be a day of the week. I have a friend called Sunday Tinubu."

"Does 'Igbinedion' mean anything to you?"

"Well, yes. It's a surname, of course, but very famous. Gabriel Igbinedion is a famous Nigerian businessman, a billionaire and philanthropist, and I think he might be the Esama of Benin, a sort of civic leader. There are always stories about him in the press."

"Oh, OK—showing my ignorance."

"Well, you're not from Nigeria, are you? I'm sure you know a lot more about Scotland than I do." They both laughed, although it was not really funny. "I'm sure it's not an uncommon name, though. There must be plenty of other Igbinedions, I think."

"How about 'Adefolake' then?" Jenny tried again, since she had started this.

"Ah, that's …" Edith began and then paused a moment. "That means something like 'your wealth supports us', I'd say."

"Interesting!"

"Yes, but remember these names are given at a very early stage," Edith said, warning against reading anything into them. "I'm not sure that any naming prophecy about an infant would be one hundred per cent accurate. If the child was called Wednesday or Born After Twins, it would tell us something. Anything else is just someone's guess or prophecy."

Jenny had had another thought. "Oh, Edith, do you know what this means?" She pushed the open book back across the counter towards Edith, indicating the wording "Akwa Akpa"?

"I think it's an area in the far south of Nigeria, near the Cameroon border, but I'm not really sure. Akwa Ibom is the name of a state down on that coast, but I think Akwa Akpa is the name of an area near Calabar, which is in the next state to the east, the Cross River State." Edith looked at the name again, written on the half title of the book, and became suddenly more enthusiastic. "Oh, wow! Where did you get this? This looks like a dedication from the author. See? 'ED', Elphinstone Dayrell."

CHAPTER 44

KALOGIROI

Tuesday, 20 August 1996, 10:40

It had seemed like a week before, but not now. Jenny knew she would have to be confident of having the final report complete on Friday—say, by lunchtime at the latest. If that meant she pretty much had to be there by Thursday evening, then she had two days after today. Today had to count, then, and the next thing she had to do was check something with Dennis Wardlaw to avoid the possibility of wasting time. She picked up the receiver with one hand as she tried to find the number with the other. Just then, there was a tap at the door. Without waiting for a reply, Katie bobbed in, an empty mug in her hand, beaming pleasantly, as usual.

"Did you have a good holiday? I know you're busy, but."

"It was lovely. Thanks, Katie. The only things to worry about were what the weather was like and if there was enough gas left to boil the kettle. The simple life!"

"And was the weather good?"

"Yes, it was mostly just about perfect. You'll always have a few ups and downs in the mountains, but it was great. It didn't hold us back and we got some brilliant climbing done."

"Bet you're pleased to be back here, then, at work and in the rain. I'll be going out to the sandwich bar and I wondered if you'd like anything."

"Oh, that would be great, Katie. I'm a bit up against it for time, so that would be helpful. Could you get me a ham and coleslaw on wholemeal and a can of Lilt, please?"

She reached for her bag, but Katie waved it away, saying, "I'll see how much it is when I've got it."

"OK. I'm just trying to pull all the last threads together, but at least it doesn't seem as though anything dramatic has happened while I've been away."

"Just the same old routine." Katie advanced towards the table.

"I was just about to call Dennis Wardlaw when you came in. If I can get a quick answer from him, it might save a bit of time."

Katie looked rather grave. "I'd try someone else, if I were you. He's just gone on two weeks' leave," she said with a smile and then picked up Jenny's mug. "This is cold. When did you last have a drink? Don't answer that—tea or coffee?"

"A coffee would be lovely, Katie. Thanks."

A few minutes later, Katie was back, a mug of coffee in one hand and a printed leaflet in the other.

"I thought so," she said, setting the coffee down on a mat. "Here you are—Kalogiroi. Dennis has this apartment there and he's always leaving these leaflets around, trying to get people to book it. It's all right for him, but it's dear for anyone else—and you still have to sort out all the flights and everything. Would you like it? There's a pile of them in the staff room."

"No, thanks," Jenny replied, adopting her business-like persona, but then she reconsidered, not so much from idle curiosity as from a desire not to seem unappreciative when Katie was being so helpful. "No, actually, yes, please." She accepted the leaflet.

Paper Chase

"Well, I'll leave you to it. See you later." Recovering her own coffee from the shelf just outside the door, Katie headed back to her desk.

Jenny did no more than glance at the printed leaflet before putting it to one side and moving to the next item on her list. Time was pressing.

CHAPTER 45

FINAL TOUCHES

Thursday, 22 August 1996, 12:50

Jenny's focus was simply on drawing all of the material together—the more difficult and anomalous matters as well as the very many more routine aspects of the exercise—and ensuring that she had done a job which was capable of standing up to the scrutiny she felt sure it would receive.

The form of her final report incorporated a schedule for a detailed management response in the form of a workplan to achieve agreed objectives within agreed timescales, dependent upon their levels of importance. In this case, although all of the more routine findings had been discussed with those directly concerned during the process, some of the more important findings had been kept under wraps, for obvious reasons. Similarly, since she would not be holding the normal "hot debrief" at the end of the audit with the senior sponsor and a few other key people, the arrangements were less transparent than she would have liked.

Normally, the report would have gone to Cameron Field, as her senior sponsor, and he would be a conduit to the board—someone who was a supporter, a translator, an advocate, thoroughly familiar with the process and the requirements.

The lack of transparency, coupled with the fact that the report would now go to all board members, meant that she wanted it to be as tight and accurate as possible.

CHAPTER
46

A COMPLETED REPORT

Friday, 23 August 1996, 14:30

Jennifer Andrews breathed a long, heartfelt sigh of relief. Her report was complete, printed, bound and distributed. She had incorporated the "Franklin" wording, which Mike Da'eth had advocated, and had left a copy for him and for each member of the board with the messenger in the mail area in the front office. Known simply as Alex (or "Old Alex", by some of the younger staff members), he handled all of the incoming and outgoing post and made collections and deliveries around the office several times a day. He knew that these items were both urgent and important, but nothing was left to chance. Each report came with a short covering letter, explaining why the report was being issued in this way by reference to the introduction to the report itself, and each was sealed in an envelope marked "Private & Confidential".

At what time would the post arrive, she wondered, and who would find his or her copy first? What precise shape would the nested ripples be as they spread necessarily, irrevocably, uncontrollably outward?

What could she say to her senior sponsor, if anything? She had asked Alex to leave his copy to be distributed on Monday morning, when the others would have theirs, rather than delivering it this afternoon.

Perhaps she could say, "There are aspects of my findings which have meant that I've had to report directly to the board, rather than having the normal end-of-audit 'hot debrief' with you, as senior sponsor."

"What aspects?" he would want to know. Had he even realised that they should be having a hot debrief today? There was nothing in the diary.

She began to clear up the remaining things in her work area. There was no great rush, as she had arranged to stay over again tonight and fly back home in the morning. The timings had seemed too unpredictable to have to rush away for an evening flight.

Sliding things into her bag or else putting them into the bin (or the shredder), she came across the Wardlaw leaflet and froze, staring at it. Kalogiroi was a seafront suburb of Limassol, just east of the centre, the other side from the military base. The bank account was with the RCB Bank in Limassol.

Simultaneously, she remembered something Brian McGregor had said in her meeting with him on the lines of "the system is designed to provide a permanent record of who did what, when".

She called his number—no reply. Then she had another thought. She buzzed through to Katie in the front office.

"Katie, did I see Brian McGregor in the building earlier?"

"Yes, he's with us now."

"Would you ask him if he can pop through and see me when he can, please? Thanks."

She turned her attention back to her desk and picked up the leaflet again, reading it and also staring through it. She called the contact number, which was international (357), presumably Cyprus.

"I am sorry, but that property is no longer available to let. We have many others, some in the same area …"

"How do you mean that one is no longer available? Do you know why?"

"I'm sorry, madam, it's simply not for let any longer."

Paper Chase

Play the sentimental card, she thought. "Oh, I really wanted that one. You see, we rented it before and wanted to go back for our anniversary."

"Yes, I understand, madam, but I'm afraid that property is on the market for sale now, so it really is not available. Obviously, we have no idea what the new owners will do. It was only put up for sale quite recently."

Jenny expressed her regret and terminated the call. She looked at both sides of the leaflet again as she gathered her thoughts.

A tap at the door and Brian popped his head in. "Jennifer, hi. Katie said you would like a word."

"Yes, thanks, Brian. Come in."

She explained that there was an unusual regular payment being made and reminded him that he had told her about the system's goal to make everything traceable. Could he find out who had actually set it up? She then moved aside to allow him to use her computer to check into this, but thought his reaction rather odd. It was almost as though he was not surprised by the dodgy payments, but was surprised that she did not know who to blame. She fed him the references and he checked again that he had taken them down properly, but he could not immediately resolve the matter.

"Try this, then." Jenny took a new tack. "Who set up the new PIN for Cameron Field? We assumed he did so himself, but the system should be able to confirm that."

A new burst of activity from Brian at the keyboard. "This has been ... but that doesn't make sense." He looked at her directly. "This shows that the second Field PIN was set up by the suppliers—at source. That cannot have been the case and yet there's only one person who could make it look like that. As head of IT, Dennis is the overall system administrator and has certain keys to access some areas of the coding."

Wardlaw, on holiday in Limassol, Cyprus, except his apartment there had been put on the market. Mysterious payments made by "Field CW", the additional ID now known (or at least strongly

A Completed Report

suspected) to have been set up by Dennis Wardlaw. The payments made to a numbered account in Limassol, Cyprus.

"I think that's all I needed to know, Brian. Thanks. Excuse me, I need to go and recover some items from the post."

That, however, was not possible. As Alex said, they picked it up early on Fridays.

Jenny came back around the corner from the mail area and could see Cameron Field in his office. He was alone and did not appear to be too busy, so—with a nod to Jean in passing—she strode in.

"Cameron, look, I completed my audit today and I wanted to forewarn you that there will be no hot debrief. Certain findings from the audit meant that I had to report directly to the board."

"What? Not for Hinton's stupid Igbin stuff!"

Mentally, he stopped dead. Was *she* the one feeding the police information? If this report went to the board over his head alleging some reasons why that was the case, he could foresee all sorts of trouble, including details getting out about his recent "involvement" with the boys in blue.

"I really don't think that's a good idea …"

"It's too late. The post has been collected and the reports have gone. But new information has just come to light to change my findings. I'm afraid the reports have already gone as written, but I'll now need to do an immediate retraction and reissue. That's what I want to speak to you about. I probably shouldn't, but the reason for not being able to talk to you seems to have gone, so I'll risk it."

"Hmm—I'm a risk, am I? I did think you had been a bit quiet, but I've been distracted by other matters."

"Look, the thing is, a false ID was set up—a second PIN on the computer system in your name—and it was used to authorise certain things."

"What!"

"Yes, including a payment of £10,000 per month for the lease of a building at Balerno Hill Trading Estate."

"Where? There's no such place!"

"Exactly. The landlord was supposed to be your partner, Jerram, and the payments were actually being made to a numbered account overseas."

"You're making this up!"

"No, I can assure you I'm not. But what I've just discovered is that all of this was done very cleverly to make it look like it was you by your head of IT."

"Wardlaw?"

"Yes. This has just come to light right now. He's supposed to be on holiday in his apartment in Limassol."

"Yes …"

"But that apartment is now up for sale and Brian is sure that he, Dennis, is the only one who could have set your second PIN and the payments up in this way. It was all based on an anomaly in the system that Brian reported to Dennis months ago and had thought no more about. He'd thought it had been taken care of, but it seems that Dennis has used the anomaly for his own ends."

"Sounds like it's been taken care of, all right!"

"I can't yet be a hundred per cent sure, but that's the way it looks. I'm trying to figure out how we check details of a private, numbered account, bearing in mind it's Friday afternoon and bearing in mind the time difference between here and Cyprus. The payments were supposed to be to J-Cash, but I suppose that could just have been a smokescreen, if the banking details for that account had been doctored anyway."

"Let me ask you one thing. Have you had any recent contact with the police?"

"What?" *(Bloody hell, what does he know?)* "Yes, my hire car was stolen before I went on holiday. I reported it at Comely Bank."

"And that's all?"

*(What **does** he know?)*

"Yes—my duty, in a case like this, is to report it to the senior sponsor of the audit. I couldn't, in this case, because it seemed as though you were implicated, so I had to go to the board. It's up to them whether they involve the police or not and on what terms."

"OK, good. What you've just told me is going to the police right now. I think they'll be interested and quite pleased to hear about this."

Flicking open his wallet, he consulted a business card with the Lothian and Borders Police crest on it and dialled a number. He got through to the person he wanted, and he was right. The police were so interested that they attended at the office very shortly afterwards, and it would be well after 7 p.m. before either Jenny or Cameron left the building.

As she was questioned, Jennifer indicated that from what she had discovered, it seemed that Cameron Field was acquainted only with a very proper and orderly loans business in J-Cash Services and that the less orderly side of it was with Jerram. She was able to speak quite authoritatively on this without disclosing the fact that her father had a loan. She did not want to get him involved any further.

When this position was reflected back to Field in separate questioning, he corroborated it. He may have taken a different approach earlier but not now, following his recent reappraisal of how his private business enterprise stood. This allowed the police to relax considerably in their dealings with him.

Jennifer also mentioned the existence of a suspected fraud, which was entirely unrelated, was at an early stage of investigation and may well later give rise to a criminal prosecution. It was with the Life Assurance Company for now—in other words, the party which appeared to have been defrauded. The police accepted this with her assurance that Field was in no way aware of or implicated in this. She stated this confidently and truly hoped it was correct.

The final day of an audit such as this could certainly be unpredictable, but now she thought her leeway of not leaving until the next morning seemed overly ambitious. She would postpone the flight and spend the morning working out what she needed to do to change her final report to make it reflect

Paper Chase

the position, as it was now known, and to try to remove any slight on Cameron Field in connection with the second ID and the Cyprus money. In view of the other loose ends there would be, she decided to stay at least until Monday. With the flurry of activity—police and otherwise—on that Friday afternoon, she had had no opportunity to discuss Igbinedion further with Catriona Rutherford at Synergy Life. She still had the files quarantined in the Morgan Field meeting room and she still held what she had been led to believe was the only key.

By the time Jenny left that evening, she had already called the offices of all of the intended recipients of her report—the board members (other than Cameron, who was, of course, already aware) plus Mike Da'eth—and left messages, either with personal assistants or with machines, to say that the report was unfortunately incorrect and the best thing to do was simply not to open it. A revised copy would be dispatched just as soon as possible, but those sent today should be confidentially destroyed. That would mean some of them would be so curious that they would read them, she thought, but she could really do no more.

Leaving the police to deal with matters concerning Dennis Wardlaw (apparently on holiday, though they strongly suspected that there was more to it) and Jerram (with whom they had apparently been unable to make contact for some time), Jenny said goodnight and left for her hotel. There, she sat in her room with an almost untouched glass of wine on the table in front of her and made notes for forty minutes.

Next, trying to imagine that the process had been cathartic, she went out for a late dinner, doing her very best to forget all about everything until the next morning.

CHAPTER 47

TIME TO LEAVE

Monday, 26 August 1996, 13:15

By lunchtime on Monday, Jenny had completely revamped and reissued her report, to allow for the new facts. It had been confirmed that the bank account in Limassol was Wardlaw's, but almost every last cent had been recently withdrawn. Later, she received positive feedback from her boss, Mike, over the report, despite the obvious embarrassment of issuing an incorrect report and then following it up with a corrected one.

Then, Lothian and Borders Police got in contact with her again. They had apparently heard from Synergy Life—whether they had actually instigated the dialogue, she never found out—and the Igbinedion matter was now the subject of a criminal investigation. She spent most of Monday afternoon with them and Catriona Rutherford in her office—that is, in the Morgan Field meeting room in George Street—after which the police took charge of the files. They left first and Jenny then escorted Catriona to the lifts. Returning to her room, she picked up her few remaining things and locked the door behind her. She went through to the main office to give the key to Cameron and say her farewells. At 5:40, the place was almost deserted, but Brian McGregor came out of Cameron's office as she arrived. He said nothing but waved a hand in such a way that she was not quite sure whether it was a greeting or something for him to hide behind. Oddly, she thought he looked close to tears.

She continued into Cameron's room. "Here's the key to the meeting room. It's locked." She put it on his desk. "The police have taken away all of the Igbinedion files, but I think it will be mostly between them and Synergy now. Well, it's been ... interesting. Sorry I couldn't have found out about the Wardlaw thing before the reports went out, but they'll all have the corrected version in the morning and hopefully will have been too busy to do anything other than destroy the first one, as requested."

He looked as if he was about to speak once or twice but said nothing. He just kept nodding his head and seemed to be making a conscious effort to look affable. Jenny's impression was that he had read both reports—of course, he alone had already received the second version—and understood.

She left and made her way back—to the hotel, to the airport, to London and hopefully to home and more normal life.

CHAPTER 48

REPARATION

Monday, 26 August 1996, 17:10

From something Jean had said, Cameron had put together what she had told him of Brian's bereavement and the story of a suicide, which the police had mooted when trying to beef up their claim of loans being made to inappropriate people. Knowing that Brian was in the building, he had asked Jean if she would arrange for him to come in.

"Brian, thanks for coming in. Sit down." He looked tense, Cameron thought. "Jean has told me about your brother. I'm very sorry. I feel I have a degree of responsibility. I don't know if you're aware, but I have an involvement in J-Cash Services, helping to fund and facilitate the business." This did not appear to be a surprise. If anything, he sensed a bitter reaction. "I really believe there is a need for a service such as this, but it has recently come to my attention that everything was not being transacted in accordance with the agreed business model. One of the prerequisites of that model was that loan recipients should be in employment and should have every expectation of being able to repay the loan. I now have to accept that I may have been involved in something which was substantially different from what I thought it was."

Paper Chase

Was it his imagination, or was he getting through to this man, who now looked more sad than angry. He could do no more than continue, genuinely.

"What I would like to ask you now is, from a practical point of view, what else could be done to help in cases like that of your brother? I know it's too late for him now, and I'm sorry, but I understand he was trying to improve his lot—was taking steps to recover. What could be done for people like him, assuming we had access to funds?"

Brian was emotionally confused. He wished he had been having this theoretical discussion weeks ago, when it would not have been too late. He had hated this man not only for being complicit in his brother's demise but for stealing money from his own company when he already seemed to have more than enough. He had done his best to bring him down by furnishing the police with incontrovertible evidence—or so he'd thought. And yet, it had turned out that he was not the thief. His explanation of his role in J-Cash was plausible, if a little naive, and he was sitting here apparently being both contrite and candid—and offering the possibility (more than just discussion, surely) of a different and realistic solution or at least a way of *helping*.

He had some ideas, however, and—trying hard to control his emotions (but not entirely succeeding)—they got down to an initial discussion. It would be the first of many and would lead to the establishment of the Derek McGregor Trust.

EPILOGUE

Before borrowing money from a friend
it's best to decide which you need most.

Joe Moore

Creditors have better memories than debtors.

Benjamin Franklin

Love all, trust a few, do wrong to none.

All's Well That Ends Well
William Shakespeare

"That was about it." Jenny smiled sympathetically, as if she had been very indulgent and Andrew had been very patient, but actually he had been rapt. "Jerram faded back into obscurity. The Derek McGregor Trust was a great success. But they never found Igbinedion. The doctor, Okonkwo, was arrested and charged, but they never found her. I get the impression that this current enquiry is something to do with trafficking refugees and that she is on their radar somehow again, but they're giving nothing away. They just ask questions."

"It's fascinating," Andrew mused, "but just answer their questions as best you can and leave them to get on with it would be my advice—whatever 'it' is."

"I reckon she was really the sleeping partner. That's if there was any 'really' about it with her. She had scarcely any more idea of the truth than Donald Trump has. But did I tell you she was a solicitor? The dread disease thing was just a sideline. Of course, she didn't really have to *sell* those policies; she just had to make up her clients and falsify the documentation. Well, actually, that's not true. Selling them to real people would be the easy way and those were the majority of her cases. Those policies for fictitious people were *all* likely to result in claims sooner or later, because of the opportunity and the cost and effort of setting them up. No point in paying for a policy for a non-existent person *unless* you plan to make a fraudulent claim.

"But in the law firm—I think it was Muazu and Partners—the so-called senior partner had the better legal credentials but was really a sleeping partner. She, Igbinedion, was the active one. I think she even resolved the estates of her fictitious clients through Muazu, in cases where the insurance proceeds went into probate. It was another name not directly connected to her, like Okonkwo. Of course, the firm was no longer in existence afterwards.

"Anyway, her passport was also a forgery in the end and I reckon she might actually have been Muazu. I told them that and they said they'd look into it.

"Jerram was never convicted, to the best of my knowledge. A lot of his people ended up behind bars, but if they got him it must have been later. Funnily enough, though, it was the J-Cash account reference associated with the payments to the account in Cyprus which launched a whole new line of enquiry into Jerram's affairs. This resulted in additional charges against him and significant sums of money being recovered by the police 'proceeds of crime' teams, even though the Cyprus account belonged to Dennis Wardlaw and the reference to Jerram's organisation was entirely fictitious, just part of Wardlaw's supposed camouflage. Wardlaw was caught and charged and lost a lot more than he could ever have gained."

The remaining coffee on the machine's hotplate had long since gone cold. At one point, Jenny's phone had buzzed. Seeing that it was Jenny B., she had pressed to send a standard "Can't talk just now, I'll call you back" message, so she must remember to call her later. Something about the upcoming exhibition, no doubt.

Now, there was a text from Charlotte saying she would be home in time for dinner. Jenny looked beyond the bright phone into the garden. It had clouded over and was drizzling slightly. It felt later in the day than it was.

As she had been moving towards the conclusion of her story, the pair of them had prepared a big tray of vegetables to roast and a half side of salmon, dressed in dill and fennel with just a little smoked paprika. Now, Andrew dipped into the fridge and grabbed something in each hand. With a deft twist, he opened a bottle of New Zealand Sauvignon Blanc, pouring a sensible measure into each of two glasses. He also peeled off the cling film from a dish of big olives, left over from last night, and they settled down in the comfortable chairs again.

There was one other thing which, to the best of Jenny's knowledge, the police never discovered. She herself had discovered it only some years later and that had happened in a way which ought not to have occurred, through some work she was doing in connection with several European banks—and through a certain unpardonable lack of discretion on the part of one of her colleagues.

In the autumn of 1991, during a short break in Barcelona, Cameron William Field had won just under €6.25 million on Bonoloto, a well-established Spanish lottery. Of course, the Euro had not come into being as yet; the actual win was a figure of nearly 715 million pesetas, then equivalent to roughly £3.9 million.

He had managed to avoid publicity locally and had had no wish for this story to leak out, for a variety of reasons. He had not wanted the attention and had not wanted to receive begging letters (or their equivalent). He also did not really approved of lotteries and was not quite sure what had caused him to give in to the temptation to play this one. Finally, and even apart from the other reasons, he'd had no desire to share his winnings with his estranged wife. They had been separated for just over eight years by that time, having made a clean break financially, but they had never divorced. Lilian had gone back to live in Ireland, at least initially. She was quite capable of looking after herself, in terms of earnings, and had come from a rather wealthy family, in any case. Their son, James, had been born in 1976 and so would have been 15 by that time. Cameron had not seen him since the separation.

After receiving advice to make use of the 1990 amendment to Gibraltar's Bankruptcy Act, he had set up an APT (assets protection trust) in Gibraltar, which paid him £10,000 per month from the interest. He'd retained £500,000 in hand at the time, outside of the trust fund, most of which had gone towards the purchase of his luxurious apartment (without the burden of a mortgage). Despite this initial cash deduction and the monthly payments, the interest levels were such that the amount of capital within the trust had gradually appreciated.

Apart from the upgrade to his residence, he had never really allowed this windfall to change his lifestyle. With his generous salary, which was commensurate with his position, and especially with the added payments he'd had coming in from Gibraltar, he had certainly not been badly off, but the extra cash had gone more towards expanding his onshore wealth than towards extravagances, more towards boosting his various investment accounts than towards visible illustrations of his wealth. The purchase of the holiday properties in Northern Cyprus and the arrangements made with Jerram regarding J-Cash Services had been perhaps the only exceptions to this—until, of course, the establishment of the Derek McGregor Trust.

Cameron had closed down the APT in Gibraltar and transferred the funds in their entirety to a charitable trust named the Derek McGregor Trust. He had worked with Brian McGregor in establishing both the trust and its operating parameters, which were essentially providing support for people who were in short-term financial and other difficulties, including those suffering addiction problems. Latter-day Calvinist that he was, Field had insisted on tangible signs of a desire to recover—not merely to accept support—and McGregor had fully endorsed that approach. They were both directors of the new charitable trust, but Cameron Field had given up his role with Morgan Field Associates to run it, rather than appointing a senior person to do so and thus beginning the slippery slide towards being an organisation which serves its own interests almost as much as those of its stated benefactors. He already had enough money to get by, even without his salary or the income from Gibraltar.

In the immediate aftermath, to avoid any conflict or possible variance from the parameters and priorities of the new organisation, Cameron had simply cleared the outstanding debts of the existing J-Cash Services customers, anonymously, out of his own pocket. He had arranged for a letter to be sent to each of them stating that the debt was to be wiped out on this one occasion and for other, wider reasons. It had encouraged them to use this good fortune as a fresh start and a new way forward—as a steppingstone—to try to ensure that they never again had to resort to taking on a debt of this sort. He had updated the accounting record normally supplied each month by Jerram on this basis, but with little expectation of receiving the eventual return of what remained of his original £200,000.

He had not previously been privy to the names and addresses of those customers, only to the financial details of the loans. When his reason for requiring these details had been made known to the police, however, the information had become available. He did not like to ask whether this had been done officially or not, as he suspected he knew the answer.

In reading the letter—signed only "J-Cash Services" —Jenny had noted that it bore the initials "CWF/JS" in a small, 4-point file reference at its foot. The amnesty had been an unexpected bonus for Stuart, but the letter spent many years in a frame on the wall of his daughter's study.

These were more or less the facts which had been narrated to a patient Andrew Wilson, may he rest in peace, on that Sunday morning all those years ago.

But this time, when she emerged from the story, Jenny was looking across the darkening conservatory at the son and daughter of James Field—grandchildren of Cameron—who had been trying to resolve their father's estate and had till now found more questions than answers.

She had resisted their early entreaties for information but had eventually invited them for lunch, thinking that there was really no one else who could tell them and why not? She had invited them to come on a Saturday—it was 23 November and seemed fitting. Lilian was the elder, but both she and Patrick appeared to be in their thirties.

Jenny did not know the whole story but probably knew more than anyone and what she knew she had told them. They had been especially interested in the Derek McGregor Trust, of which their father had inherited executive control but which he had never even mentioned, and in the evidence of their grandfather's fascination with West Africa.

"Your grandfather really believed in the business of providing small, short-term loans—what became known as payday loans. He was genuinely trying to meet a need which existed in society. Remember, he was basically funding it out of his own pocket. But the way it worked out, most of the loans remained outstanding over a period of months, rather than weeks and were sought not in response to a one-of item of expenditure but just to cope with routine costs—to make ends meet. And of course, the longer the loan was outstanding, the more penalising its higher level of interest rate became.

"I know it's a long time ago now, but figures I had in the earlier part of this century showed that the average value of a payday loan was less than £300. That would be probably about €1,000 nowadays—the UK pound probably isn't very representative anymore—but can you imagine having to resort to that sort of loan business for less than €1,000?"

"Yes, I know what you mean," Lilian agreed, "and that whole UK split from the EU thing was so disruptive. We were in London then. Dad was at UCL, but he just couldn't stand the idea of being in a backwater—of deliberately cutting ourselves off and sticking our heads in the sand—so we moved to France initially."

"I can understand that," Jenny put in. "After the original irresponsible referendum, my first thought was, *Where shall I go?* I thought of France or possibly Italy."

"Well, we were France. We had a beautiful old house right down on the bank of the Garonne, in Bordeaux. Dad had a position at the Université Bordeaux Montaigne, where they run courses in African studies, in conjunction with the Institute of African Studies at the Universität Bayreuth in Germany.

"After Scotland engineered a way to stay in the EU, we moved there. I was in *Le Collège* by then—a bit like middle school. I think he wanted to be back in an English-speaking place before we got much further through the education system.

"And look at things now! Who would have said that the mighty United Kingdom of England and Wales would be playing second fiddle to Scotland, as well as Ireland? At least they still have a stronger economic record than Faroe-Zetland. Their best asset seems to be the weak pound, because it makes tourism more attractive."

With a minimum of fuss or even interruption to the conversation, Jenny had contrived to bring through a tray of tea with a plate of incredibly light orange-and-almond cookies, which Lilian thought must be home-made.

"It was so odd that we moved to Edinburgh, where Dad originally grew up, or spent his early years, at least, as it had been his father telling him all the stories of West Africa, then, that had inspired his interest in the continent that would be his life's work. It seemed as though the chair just happened to come up, but I suppose he had had an eye on it for a while. It's obviously a specialist area and Edinburgh is a really well-respected centre. So, suddenly we were in Edinburgh and Dad was a professor at the university and director of the Centre for African Studies there."

Patrick took the story up. "I couldn't believe it when I found out his father was still alive and probably resident in the city. We'd never really known anything about our grandfather. I must have been 12 or 13 by then. I didn't really say anything about it at home, but I took it upon myself to find out where he lived and to make contact. It wasn't difficult, really. The hardest part was getting in to see him, because he was a bit of a grumpy old bugger at first. He soon relented, though. I think it was the look of me, as much as anything. He showed me a picture of himself when he was quite young and it could have been me."

There was a real likeness, Jenny thought.

"Dad wasn't very happy at first, especially since we had both met him by the time he found out, going behind Dad's back. But we soon managed to talk him around, didn't we? And we got the two of them reconciled before long."

And so, the two older men, father and son, had been reconciled. In fact, there had been little to reconcile. They had really required only the catalyst of youth to bring them back together again—to reintroduce them.

"They were a bit slow at first," Lilian continued. "They had not known each other for most of Dad's life and they were two of a kind, really—not exactly gregarious or what you'd call happy-go-lucky. And they had more similarities and differences than they knew at first. Dad's parents had split up when he was only seven and, not long after that, he'd gone with his mother to Ireland, which was back home for her."

"Yes, but then we found out that Dad was born six months after they got married, so maybe it wasn't the most auspicious of starts," added Patrick with a shrug.

"Dad stayed in Ireland until after he had his first degree," Lilian continued, "and then he was in his thirties, in London, when he got married. But that didn't last long either. At least there was a bit of a gap before we arrived on the scene." She cast a look at Patrick. "I was three years on and Patrick another four years later, but just a year or so after that she sort of wandered off, apparently, our mother. I can remember her vaguely, but Patrick not at all. She was always a bit of a Bohemian type, seemingly, into living in the moment and recreational drug use and not at all like Dad, really. He said, on the rare occasions when he would even mention it, that he'd heard she went to India first and then Australia, but I don't think he was ever very sure. Anyway, he and Grandad did get much closer and then it was almost as if they were trying to make up for lost time. (Almost.)"

Patrick now took up the narrative once more. "Yes, at one point Grandad said he wasn't going to change his will because of this reintroduction, but it was a bit like his idea of a joke. He said he wasn't going to change it because he'd left everything to Dad already."

"He did change it, though."

"Yes, he took advice and decided it would be more tax efficient if he left most of it to us, being a generation down, so we ended up inheriting the house between us (albeit held in trust by Dad, who had the option to use it freely throughout his lifetime) and upwards of one million euros each."

"That was back in '38," Lilian explained. "Dad still got a bit more than pocket money too, as well as his free lifetime tenancy of the house, but we just didn't know anything about this big trust fund. Dad simply never mentioned it."

"Well, at least now you do know something of the background," Jenny said. After a short pause, another thought struck her. "By the way, do you know what *Akwa Akpa* means?"

"What it *means*?" Patrick queried, as if expecting a different question.

"It's the old name for Calabar," Lilian explained, "the city which is the capital of the Cross River State in South-Eastern Nigeria. It's the original Efik name for the city—but to us, it's home. It's the name of the house we grew up in, in Hertfordshire."

Cameron had written it on the half title of the book, but it was not mentioned in any of the stories. Jenny had read that slim, well-thumbed volume from cover to cover. But there must be some significance, some other story if the son, who had known his father only in his first few years, named his house Akwa Akpa. And the father had passed this on to his son long before he'd known Adefolake Igbinedion. Jenny felt like the young Mayowa—searching.

Patrick glanced at his wrist device. "Look, we'd better be making tracks. Do you see the time?"

"OK, I'll call the car." Lilian fished out her phone.

"We can call mine."

"No, mine is closer—and it's fully charged."

By the time the pair had thanked her for lunch—and just for seeing and educating them—and had promised to call again, to provide an update on how it was all going, the car had arrived. They had arrived together by car, but Jenny did not know whose it had been. She had watched it drive off, presumably to find itself a convenient place to await a further summons.

She had thought it was so clever, back in 1996, that she'd had a telephone which could be used outdoors without having to be plugged into the wall. What changes she had seen in her eighty-one years!

She intended to see quite a few more yet, thank you very much.

Printed in Great Britain
by Amazon